Classic Swoı

The Magnificent Barbariaı
dangerous enemy—a beautiful sorceress with magic powers
and unspeakable passions.

KOTHAR

and the

DEMON

QUEEN

Book 3

by Gardner Francis Fox

Originally printed in 1969

digitally transcribed by Kurt Brugel 2017
for the Gardner Francis Fox Library LLC

Gardner Francis Fox (1911 to 1986) was a wordsmith. He originally
was schooled as a lawyer. Rerouted by the depression, he joined the
comic book industry in 1937. Writing and creating for the soon to be
DC comics. Mr. Fox set out to create such iconic characters as the
Flash and *Hawkman*. He is also known for inventing *Batman's* utility
belt and the multi-verse concept.

At the same time, he was writing for comic books, he also contributed
heavily to the paperback novel industry. Writing in all of the genres;
westerns, historical romance, sword and sorcery, intergalactic
adventures, even erotica.

The Gardner Francis Fox library is proud to be digitally transferring over 150
of Mr. Fox's paperback novels. We are proud to present - - -

Table of Contents:

CHAPTER ONE

For uncounted years the mage Mindos Omthol had lived by the side of the Sunken Sea, in a gaunt black-tower that had been built in the forgotten years when there had been water in that ancient sea-bottom. For all those years, while he had performed conjurations for the wealthy merchants and the noblemen of Thankarol and Niemm, he had dreamed of the lost spell of Baithorion, which was said to give the performer of that necromancy the lost secret of eternal youth.

Mindos Omthol was an old man, wrinkled and bent. He had few years left in which to find the lost parchments of Baithorion. His chests and coffers were heavy with the gold and jewels he had amassed over the years; he had no more need for wealth; the only thing he wanted, and needed with an almost insane desperation, was his departed youth. Here and there in the great metropoli of his world, in Romm and in Memphor, in Thankarol and in Niemm, he had agents searching relentlessly for some hint of those almost legendary scrolls.

At long last, in ghoul-haunted Anthom, which was little more than a city of the dead, an agent came across a forgotten passageway, discovered when the bricks of a cellar were knocked down to extend an aqueduct. The passageway, its floor thick with dust, its walls hidden by spiderwebs, led to a circular stone room that turned out to be a depository of much forgotten, arcane lore. Encased in an ivory cylinder were the lost conjurations of the long dead Baithorion.

With quivering fingers Mindos Omthol unscrewed the ivory cylinder and gently removed the crackling parchments. His rheumy eyes scanned the sheets of vellum, widening in disbelieving delight. At last, he had the secret of eternal youth in his hands. The sigils and scrawlings that marked these sheets were in the very handwriting of Baithorion himself!

Eagerly he set up his alembics, the great phials which contained the gore of fifty virgins, and the golden censers which held a potent incense made from dead men's bones. He planted his sandaled feet inside the red pentagram drawn with the blood of a recently deceased high priest and which Mindos Omthol himself had extracted before the high priest had been laid to rest.

In a quavering voice he chanted from the forgotten language, known these days only to Mindos Omthol himself. His hand swung the censer, his eyes beheld the gray incense smoke rising and spreading, his ears heard—

There was a rustle as of dried leather. Ahh! Something was forming in the shadows beyond the pentagram, where all was black as ebony out of the jungle worlds of Oasia. A living presence was shaping there, a sentience which betrayed itself at first only by two blazing red eyes.

The spell of Baithorion was working! His old heart thudded inside his rib cage as the mage leaned forward, looking toward those glaring orbs. "Are you. Abathon? The demon of the ten hells of Kryth?"

"I am Abathon," was a whisper in the blackness. "Who summons Abathon from his eternal pleasures?"

"Mindos Omthol, the magician of Niemm."

"What would you of Abathon?"

"Youth! I want—youth a strong young heart, a powerful young body to enjoy the wealth and knowledge I have amassed over the years."

There was a little silence. When the demon spoke, it was with obvious reluctance. "Dread and dangerous are the spells of Baithorion! Be warned, mage. Better to let Abathon go back to his pleasures in awesome Kryth than to dare what has been forbidden for all men to know since Baithorion died in screaming madness. Let me go, I say, and I shall forget what—"

"No!" shouted Mindos Omthol. His scrawny hand reached for a vial of virgins' blood. With a scream of lust greater than the lust of any man for any woman, he hurled the glass vial across the room, past the red mark of the pentagram and at the shadowy thing that was red-eyed Abathon.

The vial was deftly caught. The demon breathed in the smell of the blood and was lost. Muttering, "Long have I gone unfed on nectar such as this," he raised the vial to his grotesque mouth and drank.

"You must serve me now," the mage screeched, dancing in his triumph. "You have drunk the blood, you have committed yourself to my command."

The demon did not answer, being busy with the vial. His long tongue came out to lap away the last traces of that red substance and then he lowered the cruet.

"I have drunk the blood. I am yours to command," he said simply. Yet to the mage, there seemed to be a hesitancy about Abathon that put him on his guard.

"Make me young. Eternally young—like Baithorion!" he shouted.

"Not so fast. Young I can make you, but only for an hour. You see, there is a—"

"No," screamed Mindos Omthol angrily. "The spell is for eternal youth! I have read of it in the books of Gronlex Storbon, in his Dialogue of Demons and in his scarce Nights of Necromancy, which I possess. The spell is for eternal youth."

The demon snorted. "As if Gronlex Storbon knew everything! He knew little of the magician who was Baithorion. Ten times ten thousand years lay between their lifetimes. Gronlex Storbon worked from manuscripts as dusty as that from which you read! Some words he could not understand, some words were erased by the brush of Time that destroys everything.

"I, Abathon the demon god of Kryth, tell you this, that to complete your spell you need the aid of the god Xixthur."

The mage licked his thin blue lips. His heart, which had sunk with despair, now beat madly with renewed hope. His shaking hand he raised, to point at the horror crouching in the corner of his solar. "Tell me, how may I raise this god Xixthur?"

"By stealing him."

Mindos Omthol goggled. "Steal a god?"

"Xixthur is owned by Queen Candara of Kor. He rests within her most private bedchamber, to which she admits no one but herself—not even her lovers. In this room, hidden away at the very topmost chamber in the highest tower in the city of Kor, is Xixthur."

"I cannot enchant the god away from her?"

"Candara is part woman, part demon. She knows protective spells herself, with which she shelters Xixthur. No, no, Mindos Omthol. You cannot perform any known incantation which will release her hold on him."

"Then—then how can I get him?"

"Only a demon can steal the god, a demon who seeks the god for himself, not for any living man. And so I am afraid your quest is useless. If you should ensorcell up a demon, and order it to steal Xixthur for you, he would fail because he would not be stealing the god for his own use."

"No, I am afraid you have wasted your time. However. . . "

"Yes?" quavered Mindos Omthol hopefully. "There may be a way. I can sense the conjunction of strange and eerie forces in your world. I seem to see the figure of a man striding across the mists of the Haunted Lands, a man with a great sword."

"What do I want with a man?" snorted the baffled mage.

"Do not scorn that which you do not understand! I see also, in the city of Urgal an old, old demon—a demon even older than you, magician. His strength and powers are on the wane. He may do you a favor —and steal the god Xixthur for his own use."

Mindos Omthol clapped his old hands. "Then you can steal Xixthur away from him? Is this what you are telling me, Abathon?"

"Know you anyone who can rob from a demon? No, no-don't ask me to do it. I do not prey on my own kind. You must find another."

The sorcerer wailed, "But what else is there but demons who can help me? My agents are no help, they possess neither the strength nor the will to steal from demons. And as for the race of men—bah!"

Abathon chuckled. "The man I see in the mists is big and strong, Mindos Omthol. He carries, a magic sword. It may be that he—might help."

The magician needed no further hint. He whirled toward a great crystal globe, making sure not to step beyond the red lines of the sacred pentagram, for then Abathon would be under no compulsion to serve him, despite having drunk the blood of the fifty virgins; and might attack and destroy him, treachery being the main characteristic of all demons.

His withered hands made cryptic signs above the crystal, his mouth uttered harsh, blasphemous words. His old eyes watched as the crystal grew less clear, turned cloudy and became the mists of the Haunted Lands.

Mindos Omthol stared at a figure of a giant youth, small inside the crystal but huge by comparison with the stone blocks past which he walked, leading a gray horse. He wore a mail shirt that glittered as if newly polished, there was a leather kilt about his loins, and a great sword with a red gem set into its hilt bobbed at his side. A yellow mane of uncut hair hung down to his shoulders, hair that blew this way and that to the strong winds sweeping the barren plains of the wasteland through which he moved.

"Is this the man?"

The demon nodded. "I sense strange powers about him. If I knew not better I would say he is under the protection of Afgorkon himself, beside whose arcane wisdom even Baithorion was but a babe, while you yourself might as well not have been born."

At sound of that dread name, Mindos Omthol made a protective sign with his fingers in the air. He wheezed, "If Afgorkon protects him, what use is he to me?"

"Afgorkon sleeps, at times. If you dare . . ."

Mindos Omthol gibbered in his eagerness. "I dare, I dare," he cried, leaping from one foot to the other. "I dare anything to be young once more. Tell me what to do, Abathon. Tell me!"

The demon began to speak.

Kothar had walked for hours through the white mists of the Haunted Lands. Beside him were the gray stone blocks which, rumor said, had been used to build the lost city of Dru in the days of its greatest glory, half a million years before. The barbarian swordsman was not interested in lost cities; his belly was too empty for that, he needed food badly.

It had been a hare-brained impulse that had brought him across the Rooftop of the World and down those mountain slopes into the Haunted Lands where lived demons and ghouls who ate the flesh from a man's bones even while he was still alive. Kothar was fleeing from the thought of Red Lori, the sorceress who hated him and whom he had imprisoned in the tomb of Kalikalides and sealed therein with solid silver along the edges of the mausoleum door. He had ridden away, leaving her a prisoner with the lich of dead Kalikalides, and Kothar felt vaguely uneasy about the whole thing.

8

Oh, yes. He had tricked her. But since then Red Lori had been silent. She had not appeared to him in the ale cups he had downed in the taverns of Balthogar and Romm on his way toward the high mountains known as the Rooftop of the World, nor even in the fires he set at night in his lonely camps. And this was the way of Red Lori, so that Kothar had become accustomed to it, ever since Queen Elfa of Commoral had put Red Lori in a silver cage and hung her in her audience hall.

It had been Kothar who had captured Red Lori, the sorceress. It had been Kothar who had stolen her naked body out of the silver cage to save the life of Mahla, daughter of old Pahk Mah. He had ridden into Memphor where the mausoleum of long-dead Kalikalides stood, so that Red Lori could recapture her lost magics.

Now he was fleeing from his memories. At any time he expected to see the woman of the red hair step out from behind a boulder and confront him. His palm itched and burned to grasp the pommel of his sword Frostfire and test its steel against her woman-flesh Yet she did not appear, neither in mist nor ale cup nor campfires, and so Kothar, worried.

"It isn't like her," he muttered to his gray warhorse, Greyling. "She should be cursing me up and down and through the middle. And she's silent. What evil can she be cooking up?"

The big gray shook its head and silver mane, making its ring-bits jingle. Kothar rumbled laughter. "You don't know either, do you? Still, we'll both be on our guard."

All men of Yarth hated and feared the Haunted Lands, through which the blond giant strode. There were devils and worse in these mists that seeped eternally from cracks in the rocks and crevasses in the ground, and that came down from the very clouds to add their moisture to the rest. A wanderer might make only a weak fire in this wilderness of tumbled stone and gravelly ground. It was a dead, barren world, and what little vegetation grew here was sparse and stunted, and oddly distorted.

Men said there was a city in the Haunted Lands. Its name was Kor. Its queen was beautiful Candara.

Kothar had hopes of finding Kor, of taking service with Queen Candara, whom men said was a demon. Demon or woman, it made no difference to the blond barbarian so long as she paid her soldiers in good gold. And gossip had it that she did this, robbing the gold from the merchant caravans that skirted her borders in abject terror.

The mists appeared to be thickening around him, the deeper into the Haunted Lands he went. They billowed and eddied in the wind. From time to time the Cumberian fancied he could see faces there, and that he could hear voices warning him to go back, go back, this land was not for him.

Kothar grinned coldly. Maybe this was why Red Lori was letting him alone. He was walking toward a fate more awful than any she might conjure up for him.

Now he heard strange sounds, like wet mud being squelched and trodden as if by some mighty beast. Kothar held his breath, listening. He turned suddenly and caught at Greyling, pressing his hands to its nostrils that it might not whinny out its fear.

"Easy, easy," he begged.

"By Dwalka! We're in a very hell, inside this place. Be quiet, Greyling—on both our lives."

He dropped the reins, knowing the warhorse would wait patiently and silently for his return. On war-booted feet he moved forward, drawing Frostfire from the scabbard with but a whisper of steel on metal.

Past a huge boulder that bore cryptic carvings, put there by a hand that Yarth had long ago forgotten, he inched his way over wet stones and a pallid moss that grew between them. Inside him, he knew, a primeval fear, the fright man has always had before the unknown, the mysterious. His mighty fingers tightened on his sword-hilt.

A wind blew up, moaning about his ears. The mists eddied around him, parting. There was a dark something beyond those mists, half glimpsed, half hidden by them. A gigantic something that moved, that made those squelching noises. Kothar felt the hairs on the back of his neck stand up. In the name of his Northland god, Dwalka—what was this thing?

It towered up, higher than a city wall. It was black and scaly, and its bulk was ten times greater than a house. It was the size of a small palace! Kothar choked back a curse.

The beast-dragon behemoth—paused as if the wind that shook the mists carried with it his man-smell to its nostrils. A great mouth yawned, disclosing huge teeth. And then its bellow shook the ground beneath Kothar's war-boots

Sweat stood out on his brow. He dared not move, he was frozen motionless. Slowly Kothar backed, until his spine was touching the side of a huge gray boulder. The beast could not swallow him and the rock, not together. His fingers tightened his grip on the Sword-hilt.

The beast moved its head from side to side, questing for that elusive scent. Tiring of its pastime, it moved on through the noisome swamps, feet lifting from the mud and water with those loud, squelching sounds.

Kothar heaved a sigh. "By Dwalka! This is no place for us to be, Greyling."

Catching up, the reins of the terrified beast, he moved on carefully, walking always on the firmest sections of ground where the greenest grass grew, for a misstep in any other direction might mean their deaths. For miles they walked, the big man and the warhorse, but at length the mists fell away to reveal the slopes of distant hills and a grassy plain between.

Kothar swung into the saddle and rode. Kor lay beyond the hills, not far away. In other lands, the name of Kor was dreaded and reviled. It had been founded many centuries ago by mutinous soldiers from Avalonia and Vandacia, together with a mixed crew of criminals and riffraff out of Commoral carrying the leopard banner of an exiled queen named Candara. There were women with the men, camp followers and harlots who were themselves thieves and cut-purses.

Such as these had laid the first stones of Kor, with the help of a god, some men said, named Xixthur. It was the largest city in the haunted lands, there were few who dared attack it. And so, in its way, it prospered. Oddly enough, Kor had always been ruled by a woman whose name was Candara.

The first Candara had been sister to the king of Vandacia. The demon served her whim, history said, and had suggested that she flee away from Vandacia with its malcontents and rebels to set up her own realm. She was reputedly a beautiful woman, dusky of skin with hair the tint of a blackbird's wing, and glossy, with eyes that resembled the black of pure obsidian.

Kothar came through the hills at sunset. Below him lay the plain of Kor and on it lay the city. It was a vast, walled place with leaden roofs alternating with red tiles and blue, the houses themselves being of gray stone. The barbarian stared down at Kor and grimaced. Leaning over the saddle, he spat in disgust.

"A vile place, that stinks," he growled. "My better judgment tells me to ride on, to skirt those walls. But my belly is empty, needing food, and my mouth would not object to a washing down with ale."

He grinned at the thought, and straightened. He was becoming an old lady! He supposed it had to do with Red Lori, whom he had left sealed up in the tomb of dread Kalikalides to share eternity with the dead mage. He had been uneasy about it, ever since.

His war-boot toed Greyling to a canter. The sun was setting behind his back as it lowered over the peaks of the Roof of the World. Shadows were long and ominous as the gray horse cantered between the huge wooden gates which men were beginning to close even now, while there was still light on the plain of Kor by which to see.

Kothar asked, "A good inn? That doesn't rob a man?"

An officer in worn armor waved an arm, grinning. "The Queen's Navel, on the first street to your left past the square. Good supping, stranger!"

The Cumberian thought it a bit odd that he was not interrogated more thoroughly; he was a stranger and well armed with a long-sword at his side and a horn bow and quiver on his horse, but he guessed Kor welcomed whatever visitors it might get, for it was not a pleasant place to be.

The air smelled of wine and garbage, since this was the windless season, and the mists came up to the walls of the city like an attacking army every night, as if to pen those stinks inside. Kothar blew his nose and toed Greyling to a faster run.

As he moved down the Street of Wine-sellers and away from the gate square, the air became fresher, sweeter. His eyes sparkled. Lovely women moved along the narrow walks, hips swinging, and sometimes one or two of them turned to smile at the huge blond stranger. Doors opened onto common rooms where the fragrance of baking bread mingled with that of roasting meats and freshly sliced cheeses.

Kothar grinned, coming to a sign that showed the supposed belly of the queen, and a deep-set navel. There was a tiny stable to one side of the inn, which a man, could reach by walking below a wooden archway into an inner court.

A boy ran to snatch the reins of the warhorse and catch the copper coin Kothar flipped through the air at him. He nodded when the barbarian told him he wanted good oats, clean water, and a dry place for Greyling to rest.

Kothar lifted a muscular arm, pushed open a door.

He did not see the thing in black rags that snuffled and lurched along the corridor to his right. It stiffened at the scent of the Cumberian, lifting its head almost out of the hood of the tattered cloak that hid its body. Red eyes blazed at sight of the young giant, and what seemed to be a forked tongue ran slowly about its lips.

With something of a limp, it turned and scurried for the darker shadows of the street. The patter of its feet made oddly metallic sounds.

Kothar strode into the common room, into the smells of bread and meat and cheese. A dozen men turned their heads at sight of him; they were burly men, coopers and wainwrights and a blacksmith or two. Their eyes held steady as they scanned him. He read neither friendship nor enmity in their eyes. A woman stepped from around a wooden tun which a man in a leather apron was broaching, and advanced on him.

"Where'll you sit?" she asked.

"Is there a difference?" he wondered, intrigued.

She waved a bare arm to her left. "Over there's where the girls come to dance. A strong man like you can get the woman of your choice if she must pass by you, instead of running across half the room." She turned and gestured to her right. "That's the place where the food is served. We make plenty but there are always men to eat it and to drink the ale and such whiskey as we serve, and there are some who may take it away from you."

The woman laughed, her eyes flirtatious. She was pretty enough, but a little old and shopworn for Kothar, though there were times when he would not have scorned her body in his bed. A simple tunic covered her body from shoulders to knees and was held at her middle by a broad leather belt.

13

"So which is it, my young giant? Food? Or Women?"

Kothar grinned. "Sit me where the women walk. I can always get what food I need. And right now, I need plenty."

The woman said softly, "Don't be too sure about the food. The men who come to the Navel are strong and fearless. They fear nothing, except perhaps Zordanor."

"Who's this Zordanor?" he asked, but she had turned on a slippered heel, to march him across the room toward a small table set near an open space on the floor.

He noticed a curtain hung to one side of and almost directly behind his chair. Apparently the dancing girls came from the curtained doorway, passing by his table to reach the space where they would dance. Kothar grinned hugely. He was not thinking of wenches, but more of his empty belly; still, when he had eaten and drunk enough, he might be interested in a female.

He slipped a copper coin to the woman, who looked surprised. Then she smiled in a friendly way and said, "Pick up a platter at yonder table, go to the long counter set close to the far wall and bang on it with a spoon. I'll see that a girl attends you."

The barbarian nodded. His stomach rumbled. He growled, "Fetch me a tankard of ale. I die of thirst from a long ride."

The woman shook her head. "I seat the men, to prevent quarrels. The girl who brings you meat will fetch you ale."

She walked away. Kothar rubbed his chin thoughtfully. He was a stranger, he would follow these customs of Kor, being a polite man when it suited him. He moved like a tiger to the table filled with wooden platters and selected one, then a spoon. His dagger would serve for knife and fork.

He banged the spoon on the counter. As he did so, the door swung inward and four big men came striding in off the street. The woman hurried forward, but the men waved her away, looking hard at Kothar. They seated themselves at a table not far from the food counter.

A pretty girl with long yellow hair came running as the spoon banged. Her face was a little frightened, Kothar thought, so he tried to reassure her.

"Meat, my pretty. Roasting meat, with the blood running from it.

14

And plenty of it. With freshly baked bread and a wedge of strong cheese. And a big tankard of ale."

She bobbed her head and ran. Kothar felt the eyes on his back with the instinct of a wild animal. The skin crawled between his shoulder blades. Slowly he let his eyes roam about the room. The dozen early eaters had forgotten the food on their plates, they were more interested in him and in the men who sat at a table near the counter.

He stared at the men. They were big, heavily muscled. Their faces were pitted and scarred, and their eyes were the eyes of pigs, though merciless. He knew their kind. They hungered for amusement, and they had settled on him as the man most likely to give it to them, despite his muscular bulk.

The girl came back, holding his platter laden with newly sliced meat and bread, with a large chunk of cheese. She told him the price and he paid her in the silver dinars of Balthogar.

She scooped up the coins and ran. Kothar turned, the platter in his big hands. The four men at the nearby table were rising to their feet, grinning. They were moving apart, by two's. Kothar saw that when he walked between them, they would move in on him.

He stepped forward, as if ignoring them. One of the men said, "Put it on my table, stranger. That is just about the sort of supper I'd have chosen for myself."

Kothar lifted his eyebrows, halting. "What table is that, friend?"

The man laughed contemptuously, pointing. Kothar moved as does the hunting cat in the jungles of Oasia, gracefully and with blinding speed. The platter of hot meats he rammed into the face of his tormentor. In almost the same motion his big hand gripped the edge of the wooden table and drove it up and sideways into the bellies of the two bullies to his right. They went down gasping, with sick groans.

One man remained untouched. Him Kothar caught by the collar of his woolen jerkin and by the leather belt at his waist. He swung him upward without effort, drove him downward into the man whose face was red from hot meat and scalding gravies. Then he lifted them and slammed their heads together.

"You've spoiled my meal, the lot of you," rumbled Kothar.

The heads cracked together again. "I'm not a rich man, I can't pay for this entertainment you're giving me."

Crack went the unshaven polls. "You'll pay for my meal, you shall, and add in some fine wine to quench the thirst you've raised."

He let the men sag to the floor by opening his fingers. They lay like scarecrows placed in a cornfield to fright off the birds. Grunting, he stared down at them, then reached for a fat leather purse attached by chains to the belt of his chief tormentor. He opened the purse, grinned when he saw all the fine silver, and tossed a handful of coins on the counter-top.

"Fill me another plate, dumpling," her told the blonde girl. "And this time, add a bottle of your best wine to my mug of ale."

He carried his platter and the wine bottle to his table, and began to eat. Kothar was possessed of a barbarian's prodigious appetite, he relished every mouthful as if it might be his last. He drained his mug of ale, then scorned a glass to tip the wine bottle to his lips and drink.

By this time, the four men were stirring, rising to their feet and looking blearily about them. Kothar waved a big hand.

"Come sit on the floor at my feet, dogs. I don't want you baying to the street watch about my having stolen your silver."

The men advanced on him with a hangdog air. One of them blustered, "You can't keep us sitting at your feet, stranger."

"Sit," said Kothar, and the men sat. When the bottle was almost empty, the Cumberian said, "I thank you for the gift of dinner. It tasted especially good because it was your coins that made it possible."

"You robbed my purse," said one of the four.

"It was a gift, friend, to make up for my meal you spilled. You gave me the silver with a free hand and a generous heart."

The man at his feet saw the cold bleakness of the eyes that glared down at him. His mouth went dry and he nodded, "It was a gift, freely given," he nodded.

Kothar tilted the bottle to his lips, He was in the act of draining the last bit of wine when the unnatural silence of the tavern alerted his animal-like senses. He glanced about him casually, and discovered two newcomers standing just inside the tavern doorway.

One of the newcomers was a man, misshaped with a huge hump to his back and a crouch to his stance. Shaggy hair hung below his shoulders and his wide gash of a mouth was rimmed with bulging purple lips through which a forked tongue showed as it ran about his mouth. He wore filthy rags, but the eyes that peered out from that grotesquerie of a face were bright and intelligent.

Beside this human travesty stood a woman, garbed in black hood and robe so that only her face and sandaled feet showed. Kothar stared into her face, seeing a sultry loveliness, dusky skin and a few strands of glossy black hair and large eyes in which the black pupils seemed like coals out of Hell.

She stirred faintly under his stare. "Is this the one, Zordanor?" The misshapen thing nodded its shaggy head, "The prophesying sticks said two men would come to Kor and that one of them would be of service to you. This is the other."

"Yes, the Makkadonian we already have." Kothar felt his belly muscles tense. This woman and that monster beside her meant no good to him. He might have to use Frostfire on them before he could win free. He waited warily as the woman walked toward him, the black woolen robe faintly swinging to her stride. There was something so essentially female about her walking that his eyes tried to burn through the black wool to see her body.

She said, "I will hire you, stranger."

"I came to serve Candara the queen, lady."

"Fool! Who do you think I am?" Kothar grinned. "All the queens I ever knew came with retinues of servants and many soldiers to protect them and enhance their glory."

Her laughter rang out. "I need no protection with Zordanor beside me. And being Candara, I have all the glory I can possibly use. Everything inside the walls of Kor is mine,"

"Excepting only me." Her black eyes brooded at him. "If you take my gold, you belong to me, stranger. Well? Do you accept my service?"

She made a gesture with a ringed hand. The hunchback put a paw into a velvet purse hanging at his side and lifted out a dozen gold pieces. He dropped them casually on the tabletop.

"A pledge of my generosity," the woman breathed.

The barbarian stared at the gold, remembering the three copper soltars in his leathern almoner, which was all his wealth. He nodded his blond head, and put out a hand to gather in the coins.

"Aren't you interested in the sort of employment I offer?"

Broad shoulders lifted and fell. "One task is much like another, when queens select them. I do what I'm paid to do." He picked up the gold pieces, one by one, rubbing them between forefinger and thumb before dropping them into his own purse.

"Come with us," Candara said, and turned on a heel.

Kothar went after them, tossing his cloak about his shoulders against the night chill beyond the tavern walls. He towered above the hunchback and the woman, and he wondered, as the wind came down the street and blew against his wine-warmed cheeks, if he had been hired as a bodyguard.

The woman ignored his presence, walking with her regal stride over swill-wet cobblestones and past little stone ditches filled with slops and water. The hunchback hobbled along at her side, ignoring the barbarian as totally as did Candara herself.

They came to a broad oaken gate set with brass studs, that formed the only opening in a graystone wall. Two men in armor nodded to the queen and opened the doers. They went into the outer court yard of the palace of Kor, that was bounded by a high stone wall and towered high above the smaller, meaner hovels of the citizenry of the city. Here the air was sweeter, and the torches flaring in their iron holders showed neat paving stones. Some soldiers in half-armor stood at the open armory door and stared at the little cortege. Kothar fancied he could read fear and something of sympathy in their eyes when they looked at him.

They went up a narrow stone staircase and through a wooden door into a stone chamber hung with heavy brocade draperies. A fire below a hooded chimney made a warmth in the room. A large chair was perched beside the hearth, and across the room, beside a prie-dieu holding a psaltery, was a writing desk and chair.

Candara seated herself in the easy chair. She threw back her hood. Kothar stifled a grunt of sheer admiration. By Salara of the bared breasts! This was one beautiful woman. Her face was dusky of skin, like that of a woman of Memphor, and her hair was the color of a raven wing, black and glossy, and fell to below her shoulders. Her mouth was red as newly spilled blood, and seemed made for kisses.

"Have you ever fought a demon, stranger?"

"Now and again," the Cumberian shrugged. Her laughter rippled out. "You do not fear them, then?" She leaned forward, holding her breath as she awaited his answer.

"I avoid them when I can. I fight them when I must."

"I would order you to go to the city of Urgal and either kill the demon that protects it—Azthamur—or steal from it that which Azthamur robbed from me."

"Then I shall obey."

"Or die in the attempt?"

Kothar shrugged. The queen ran her eyes over his muscular bulk and the Cumberian fancied that he could read desire for his barbarian body in her stare.

He wondered if her lust was fed on the thought that he might be a dead man in a few days.

"There is one thing. I must tell you," she said slowly. "I have chosen another to do this task for me."

"Then why seek me out?"

The hunchback; who had been standing in the shadows to one side of the hooded fireplace, spoke softly. "I have recited the incantations and cast the prophecy sticks, but I cannot tell, which one."

"Send him. If he fails, I'll go," Kothar growled. She shook her head. "No. Were I to warn Azthamur that I seek Xixthur from him, he would come at night to Kor and eat the flesh from my bones. I do not—dare to do that."

"Xixthur!"

She smiled faintly. "I shall tell you about Xixthur—if I choose you to go to Urgal."

There was a promise in her eyes that, touched sparks to the hot blood beating in his veins. Kothar rumbled, "Let there be a contest, then, between this other and myself. Whoever lives, shall go to Urgal."

Candara shook her head as amusement glinted in her black eyes.

"You could never defeat Japthon in a combat, stranger. No man born of woman can do that. And yet, I know no other way to decide. Perhaps you are smarter than Japthon, who is a brute with the brains of a pig and the body of a war-god."

"Let them fight," said Zordanor.

Regretfully, as her eyes studied the handsome bulk of the young blond giant, Queen Candara nodded her lovely head. Kothar realized she believed that she was sentencing him to death.

"When do we fight?" asked the barbarian. "Within the hour. Zordanor will show you the way."

Candara rose and smiled sadly at him.

CHATPER TWO

Deep within the pile of stone that was the palace of the queen in Kor was a small round chamber with a dirt floor and a tier of several seats rising upward from a ten foot wall around the small arena. More than a hundred torches glowed along the wall, so that the arena itself was lighted brightly while the tier of seats was in dark shadows.

Kothar came out of a doorway in the round stone wall, carrying Frostfire and a shield that Zordanor had handed him. He stepped onto the hard packed dirt and let his stare range upward toward the box bearing the royal arms, a spotted leopard rampant on an azure field. Candara sat there, shrouded in her black woolen robe, though the hood was down to show her glossy hair and her exquisitely beautiful face.

A clang of metal alerted him. He swung about as the largest man he had ever seen stepped from a dark doorway behind a raised iron grille. The man was a Makkadonian, with auburn hair beneath a high-crested helmet, wearing a mail shirt to his middle thighs and below that, red leggings strapped with brown leather. He towered half a foot above Kothar, and Kothar was himself a giant, while his arms were each a foot longer than those of the barbarian.

Kothar grunted. He had his task cut out for him, to stay alive this day. No pampered city soldier, this one; he was what the queen had named him: a brute. There was brutish intelligence beneath the shaggy brows, glinting out at him from dull blue eyes, but no wit, no understanding of anything beyond his own muscles.

Japthon let out a bull bellow and charged. In either hand, he carried a gigantic battle-ax, huge weapons made especially for his titanic strength. He swung one ax, Kothar raised his shield to block it and was rocked back on his heels by the sheer power of the arm that swung it. At almost the same moment, the other ax darted for his skull.

Kothar rasped a curse and ducked. He swung the glade in his hand, watched Japthon cross his right arm over to catch the blow on the flat of his ax-helm and deflect it. Japthon brought his left hand ax upward toward Kothar's jaw.

The barbarian leaped back, feeling shame that he must yield before the awesome strength of this other man. The shame ate in him, gnawing away even as he strove with shield and blade to turn the frightful blows raining at him from either side.

Back he was pushed, and back until his spine felt the round stone wall beyond which he could not go. The Cumberian knew the black eyes of the queen were blazing down at them and thought of the promise in those eyes when Candara had looked at him.

Slowly the shame turned to anger, to that barbarian madness with which he was wont to fight. His teeth gritted together and his lips writhed back. Though he was a giant in strength and statue, this man who opposed him was a freak in his musculature. Ambidextrous, he used either hand equally well and his great battle-axes were like darting steel petrels that would slay if they could penetrate his defenses.

Kothar lunged, driving his point straight before him. He caught Japthon poised for a double swing. The monster could not move quickly enough to prevent that steel from stabbing into his side.

The Makkadonian howled in fury. Blood came out where Frostfire had sheared through chain-mail and the cotton hacqueton beneath it, so that his mail ran red and the leather thongs that held his leggings changed their tint to scarlet. The wound was not deep but it would bother Japthon.

Japthon leaped, both axes swinging. Kothar retreated, parrying every blow. He would exhaust the bigger man, cause the loss of blood to weaken him. It was folly to stand toe to toe with him and let mere chance decide the battle by a lucky blow. Better to give ground, to let the Makkadonian tire himself.

This time, Kothar chose the way of his retreat, avoiding the round stone wall, keeping empty air at his backbone and using Frostfire as a shield. The shield Zordanor had given him was a mass of crushed wood and ripped steel, somewhere on the arena floor. Above his head, he could hear Candara crying out words, but he could not understand them.

The blows came more slowly, now. The fire was running out of the bigger man with each beating of his heart that forced the blood from the torn flesh in his side. There was a glaze over the hard blue eyes that stared at Kothar.

When he was just below the royal box, Candara leaned far out and shouted down at the Cumberian.

"Do not kill him, barbarian! He's too good a man to die like this. I will keep him as a bodyguard and send you to Urgal."

Kothar lowered his great blade, but Japthon would have none of it. The man had never met defeat, he would not accept it now. He came forward, swinging his axes for the killing stroke.

The Cumberian lashed out with Frostfire. Through a wooden haft he drove his blade, splintering it so that the ax-head fell thudding to the ground. He stabbed sideways, saw his point drive into the bulging muscles of an arm, watched the blood well and spurt.

Japthon let go his ax! He stood staring at Kothar with wide, disbelieving eyes.

He growled, "Kill cleanly, man!" His head lifted. His blue eyes blazed up at Candara. Kothar leaped, his blade flashing like blood in the red torch-lights! The flat of the blade took the bigger man on top of his head, making a sodden thunk. A moment Japthon stood upright, then slowly toppled backward, the senses knocked out of him.

Candara was on her feet. "I told you not to slay him!" she screeched. "I dazed him only," Kothar bellowed back.

"Fetch your leech, he'll have him good as new by morning—or almost."

Anger at this female crowded out his barbarian sense of caution. He growled, "If you think so much of him, let Japthon go to Urgal. I'll be gone from Kor by dawn!"

The fury faded slowly from her face. She shook her head, "No, stranger. You go to Urgal to do battle with Azthamur."

"And when I get this Xixthur for you?" She waved a ringed hand. Two men in chain-mail came to the wooden door and beckoned to him. Candara called, "Come to my bedchamber, stranger. There I shall tell you about Xixthur—and why I want him back."

Kothar shrugged and sheathing Frostfire, followed the soldiers out of the arena. As he walked along a corridor, a man carrying the little black sack of a leech hurried past him to attend to Japthon. The soldiers brought him up two flights of stairs to a door before which two burly men, heavily armed, stood guard.

One of the guards opened the door. Kothar stepped into a huge room dominated by a great four-poster bed, the coverlets of which were pale blue satin. There were lounges and cushions thrown about the chamber, the air of which was lightly perfumed. Tall windows peered out over Kor toward the misted Haunted Lands. Kothar stared out at those distant mists, remembering the beast he had encountered, and shivered.

"What? Afraid after the fighting is over?" Candara stood in a doorway leading from the bedchamber into a small anteroom. She still wore the black wool robe, with the hood thrown back, and behind her, the barbarian could see Zordanor.

She came into the room, loosening the clasps of the cloak, letting it slip from her shoulders downward. Kothar goggled. The queen was naked under a thin black thing that only pretended to hide her from neck to sandaled feet. It was a nightdress of some sort, he guessed, and its gossamer was stitched with golden threadings in cabalistic fashion.

Zordanor closed the door behind her, remaining in the outer room, leaving Candara alone with her champion. She saw the manner in which his eyes ran over her shapely legs and curving hips; and she laughed a little, as if this worship were her due.

"What reward will you ask for bringing Xixthur to me?" she murmured.

"A hundred gold pieces," he growled. Her thin black-eyebrows rose. "So little? I was prepared to pay far more."

Her hips swung lazily, challengingly, as she moved past the barbarian to a little table of ebony inlaid with ivory. An iron casket rested on its top. With a ringed hand, the queen threw back its cover.

Kothar saw that the coffer was filled with bright golden coins. Candara turned and stared at him. "This is but a partial payment, stranger—if you succeed in your venture."

The Cumberian eyed the gold with mingled feelings. The curse of Afgorkon was still on him, he knew. So long as he carried the great sword Frostfire, which was a present from that long-dead necromancer, he could own no other treasure. To Kothar, who was a fighting man above everything else, Frostfire was enough treasure to own. Yet he did not deny that so much gold would weigh heavily in his money-purse.

He sighed, knowing that this wealth could give him everything he might ever need, plenty of fine food, enough ale and wine to quench his thirsts, a woman or two to occupy his bed of nights. He was a simple man, and so he was honestly surprised when the queen spoke again.

"You might win a crown, Kothar—and me to go with it," she said softly, lifting her bare arms and stretching, moving her fully curved body from side to side beneath the thin black gossamer, so that he saw how finely formed were her legs and hips, how full and womanly her firm breasts.

The barbarian did not laugh. He had given no thought to becoming prince of Kor, but the notion appealed to him suddenly. With this woman for his queen, he might have all the wealth any man might want, for the wealth would be in the name of Candara his queen and not in his own. It was a way of getting around the curse of Afgorkon.

He grinned at Candara, stretched out a hand to ward her.

She slid aside to avoid him, but Kothar with a woman was like the tiger when it hunted. His hand veered, changing direction. His big fingers closed down on her wrists and yanked her toward him. Against his chest he crushed her, staring down into her black eyes.

"I would make you a good prince," he murmured.

"Let me go," she commanded. "You are not yet prince in Kor! And Kor is my city."

He grinned. The softness of her perfumed skin, which he could feel as his palms slid up and down her back, was borning a hunger in the barbarian. Aye, by Salara of the bare breasts. This was a woman to keep a man warm on a cold winter night.

"You're too used to a man who stands in awe of you," he grumbled, and clapped a hand to her buttock, forcing her against him. At the same time his mouth crushed her soft red-lips. She stiffened in outraged pride, but she sensed the manhood of the big barbarian and her femininity responded to it. Her bare arms came up about his neck and her soft loins plastered their curves to his hips.

"And you aren't afraid of me, are you?" she breathed.

"Nor of those soft-muscled louts you call your guards. If you want me punished for kissing you, call them in."

"For you to slay them? No, Kothar. The demon Azthamur will slay you—horribly and in dreadful enough fashion if you fail. So awfully that even my queenly pride will be satisfied for your daring to kiss me without permission."

He kissed her again, slamming her against his hard body. When he let her go, she was shivering. Her full mouth curved into a faint smile.

"And if you succeed, if you bring Xixthur back to me, then I shall be your queen, and no harm's been done."

"Who is Xixthur?" he asked. "A god of strange shape and mien. Eternally quiet, yet possessed of powers to keep me young and beautiful for many, many years."

"You want me to capture a god?"

"Xixthur cannot harm you. He is a beneficent god, who confers long life to those who keep him.

Which is why old Azthamur wants Xixthur, of course. For eons, Azthamur has dwelt in Urgal, where he serves the lords of Urgal with grim faithfulness.

"Let me warn you of Azthamur. He may not be slain—at least if he can—no living man knows how. Yet you must find a way to slay him, or failing that, to trick him into letting you take Xixthur away from him.

"But be warned! Unless you slay Azthamur, he will follow you to the very rim of Yarth itself, to claim your life as payment for your sacrilege. Once, long ago, as the story has it, one man bested Azthamur in battle and fled away with the royal princess of Urgal, Athalia the Angelic. Azthamur went after him and in the deserts south of Vandacia, caught up with him.

"The man put up a very terrible fight, but Azthamur conquered, and whatever fate then befell the man, no one knows except the princess herself, but she went mad at sight of it. Babbling horribly, she was brought back to Urgal by Azthamur, and given to her brother who was king in Urgal. No man ever saw her again, but the legend is told that she haunts the battlements of Urgal on moonless nights, howling like the doomed spirit she is."

"Tales to frighten babies!" Her lovely shoulders rose and fell. "Perhaps. I but repeat what is known of Azthamur, so you may be warned. Do not hesitate. Slay Azthamur, if you want to go on living.

There is no other way."

"And how did the demon steal Xixthur?"

"It was a stormy night, very dark, with only the scratchings of yellow lightnings in the sky to give light to the people of Kor. Perhaps the darkness that came upon my city was the result of a demon-spell, but whatever was the reason, men and women in Kor moved in a black fog that night. I myself was inside a fog, even in this bedchamber. I could not see my hand before my face.

"Sometime on that night, Azthamur came.

"When I went next day to commune with Xixthur, as is my habit, the god was gone from the little alcove off my bedchamber, that none can enter but I."

She moved gently and Kothar freed her, to watch her walk across the room to a hanging drape that showed the many loves of Salara. Clutching a pull rope, Candara whisked back the drapery to reveal a door locked and bolted by chains and bars. The chains hung loose, the bars free of the metal slots that held them.

Candara put a hand on the iron latch; she tugged. The door swung open. Past the queen, who stood to one side of the doorway, Kothar could see an alcove walled solidly with stone, the floor of which supported a stone dais. On that dais had rested the god Xixthur. It was empty, now.

"I put spells on the chains and bars of the door," Candara said softly. "It was as if the door were wide open. Azthamur went in as freely as he might walk down a street in Urgal. He took Xixthur and left the alcove. I do not know how it was done.

"Even though I am part demon, as an inheritance from my ancestors, and know many terrifying spells and conjurations, I do not know how he managed to do it. Perhaps I do not want to know, really."

She shivered. Kothar felt the hairs on the back of his thick neck rise up, bristling. He did not care for all this talk of demons. He relished a good fight with a man, but witches and warlocks were an ilk he could do without.

And yet, it was his task to slay Azthamur. "Most demons have a weakness of a sort," he grumbled. "Has this Azthamur such a weakness?"

"None that I know." The barbarian put his hand on his sword-hilt! Ah, well Frostfire had served him at other times, in other ways against demons and warlocks. It might serve him so, once again: His gray eyes brooded at Candara, studying her flesh beneath the black gossamer. He sighed. She was a prize worth fighting a demon to win.

As if she read his thought, she smiled. "Win Xixthur, win me. It is that easy, barbarian."

She turned toward her great bed, dismissing him with a wave of her hand. Kothar chuckled and moved toward her with his catlike tread. She turned, fire in her glare.

"I am not yet your queen," she snapped. Kothar laughed, "With a man, I would demand a hand fasting on our agreement. With a woman, I ask for something else."

He swept her off her feet with a motion of his big arms and tossed her onto the bed. Then he was with her, and though she screamed at first and fought, soon enough her arms were about him and her lips drank thirstily of his kisses.

2.

On Greyling, Kothar rode through the rocky wastes that day for leagues between Kor and Urgal. The scraping of iron hoofs on stones and pebbles, the beating of the hot sun down on his chain-mail shirt, were his only companions in this vast barren world. This rocky waste was part of the Haunted Lands, which stretched from Windmere Wood in Commoral as far as the rich city-state of Sybarps. It was not a kind land, to man nor beast. Until Sunset, the barbarian rode. The black ruins of a chapel rose upward from the pebbly sands, gaunt and eerie against the redness of the setting sun. This was formerly the chapel of Blessed Randolphus, his parchment map told him when he brought it out of a saddlebag and unrolled it. There was good water here and the remains of a shed were he could stable Greyling.

He had ridden the gray warhorse from Kor, intending to leave it here, against the possibility of a sudden flight from Urgal. By a long rope he had led a big roan stallion on which he would ride into Urgal. With Greyling he would leave his horn-bow and his quiver of war-arrows.

Kothar cooked his meat over a glowing fire and sat his rump on an overturned pedestal to eat it. The cool desert winds blew through the ruins at night like the screechings of a lost soul, but the barbarian heeded them not, other than by tugging his bearskin, cloak tighter about his great body.

Next day he sat the roan as it kicked up dirt and pebbles on the way to Urgal. The roan was a good horse, the sort a wandering mercenary might own.

His possession of such an animal would not arouse suspicion.

All day long he rode, into the twilight of the day. Then, when he was about to make camp, he saw the lights of distant Urgal. They were red and tiny in the far stretches between where he stood, about to make his campfire, and the city itself, and he recalled the tales of Urgal, he had heard long ago and far away in his youth at Grondel Bay. Demons dwelled in Urgal, which was a city more wicked even than Kor, for it was ruled by Prince Tor Domnus, of whom strange tales were told.

Tor Domnus kept armed men in his palace, as did Queen Candara, but where Candara contented herself with robbing an occasional caravan, Tor Domnus sold the services of his warriors to princes in the countries beyond the Haunted Lands. If a prince wanted a man slain, that prince sought out Tor Domnus and paid his price, and soon, that man who was marked for death, would die.

For a greater fee, Tor Domnus rented out his hard-bitten soldiers by the regiment. There were many barons and smaller lords in the bordering domains of Gwyn Caer and Phalkar, Sybaros and Makkadonia, who ruled in castles won with the air of Urgalian troops. Urgal and Kor existed inside the Haunted Lands because neither was quite certain of victory in any war where the other was concerned.

As he roasted his small slabs of meat over a slow fire, Kothar pondered ways and means of entering into Urgal and spiriting out Xixthur without disturbing the demon Azthamur. A bold approach was still the best. He would ride in according to his plan and seek employment as a mercenary. Once in Urgal, he would make inquiries, learn where the demon kept itself.

He ate his meat and bread, a few chunks of cheese. His wine, in a dusty bottle that had been the gift of Candara, he tilted to his lips again and again. The warmth of the fire felt good; he inched closer to it, sat huddled before the dancing flames.

It was as he swallowed the last of the wine and was about to pitch the bottle into a small stone cairn that stood beside the fire-stones, that he heard the click of footsteps.

He whirled, Frostfire half out of the scabbard. A skeleton in female garb was walking toward him. The sound he had heard was that of her bony feet striking the stones. Kothar rasped a curse and lunged upward. Frostfire came out into the firelight.

"No need for weapons between us," said a sweet voice.

"Lich!" he growled.

"Keep your distance!"

Soft laughter rose into the night. "So, a barbarian out of the northern snowfields. A fine giant of a man, but too weak to slay Azthamur. Too small, too frail!"

"What know you of Azthamur, dead one?"

"Too much, too much! What would you know?"

"How to find him, how to slay him!"

"There is no way to slay him. Yet I could show you a way into his lair whereby you might have your chance at it."

"And your fee?"

"His death, man of the north. I wait for his death without hope, as I have waited these many centuries. None may slay Azthamur, yet I go on hoping."

Kothar gestured with his free hand at a flat stone beside the fire. "Come sit you beside me, lich. Tell me of this way into Azthamur's lair."

"I may not come near the fire. I dread the heat. I move best where the night winds blow, with frost in their touch, out here on the barrens, or on the battlements of Urgal on winter nights."

"Ahhh! You're Athalia, who was princess in Urgal long ago?"

"I am Athalia—but no longer am I the Angelic One. Nowadays—or I should say—now-a-nights, I haunt the city and the castle, seeking vengeance on Azthamur who slew my lover. I have searched and searched, but none has ever come my way with any hope of victory."

"Until now," Kothar rumbled.

"Perhaps. I always, hope. I'll do what, I can, I promise. Keep you on your way, Northman. We shall meet again."

The skeletal figure in the rotted rags turned and walked off into the night desert. Kothar stared after her. She took only a few steps, she walked as normally as any woman, yet her figure receded swiftly as if Time itself hastened her departure.

Kothar shook his giant frame. There was no sight of the lich. He went toward the spot where she had stood, but there was no mark on the stone or in the dust to show that she had been here at all. Perhaps he had dreamed it. The wine Candara had given him might have been very strong, perhaps even drugged.

The Cumberian shrugged and rolled himself up in his saddle blankets. The roan would stand guard, whinnying if any came that way. Before, he fell asleep he pulled Frostfire out of the scabbard and placed it close to his hand.

Next day at noon—Urgal being farther away than he had thought last nights—he came in through the wide city gate, slouched in the high peaked saddle. His eyes went to the sellers of trade goods just outside the city gate, to the boards on which naked dancing girls postured before the flesh-tents where they welcomed their clients, to the traders in clay urns and vases, to the vendors of fruits and meats and cheeses, to the bakers of breads and sweet stuffs.

Kothar was surprised at the size and extent of the city. Kor was tiny, compared to Urgal. Urgal was closer to the borders of Phalkar and Gwyn Caer; perhaps this accounted for the greater number of traders and merchants. Besides, it was easier for a criminal to slip through the marshes of Phalkar or over the mountain passes of Gwyn Caer and arrive in Urgal, than it was to brave the empty wastes to come to Kor.

A man in armor moved from a sentry box at sight of the barbarian, hailing him. "State your business in Urgal, man. Tor Domnus takes not kindly to wanderers without a name."

"My name is Kothar, and I'm a sell-sword out of Grondel Bay where the land is too poor and the sea too rough for my stomach. I like soft lands and soft women in my life."

The officer was staring at Frostfire. "Can you use that blade you carry? Or is it loot you stole from a better man?"

"Try me," the barbarian grunted. "Not me. I'll let Evmor do that, he handles the recruits. If you've come to join the bandits our prince calls his army, that is."

"It was in my mind when I set out for Urgal."

"Straight ahead, then, until you come to the Street of Wine-sellers Turn right and travel until you see a low brick building. That's where Evmor trains his rookies."

Kothar nodded, swinging the roan about. The officer yelled after him not to waste too much time and money in the stew-pots. Evmor might want to test his swordplay, and an unmuddled head was a necessity against a swordsman as good as Evimor.

Kothar grinned his thanks for the advice. A man in half-armor, lounging in the doorway of the low brick barracks, waved a hand toward the dark recesses of the building when Kothar drew rein and asked the whereabouts of the fencing master.

"He's yonder, teaching boys to use a sword. He's in a hot temper, I'd wait until tomorrow if I were you."

The Cumberian swung from the saddle. "Damn his temper. I come seeking employment as a soldier. If some ninny named Evmor can best me—with either fist or sword, mind—I'll go away meekly."

The soldier laughed. "Yours is the casket at the funeral, stranger. Do what you want." Kothar noticed that he pulled his shoulder from the door lintel and came after him at a distance as the barbarian walked toward a sunny spot in the open courtyard behind the brick wall.

There were perhaps half a dozen youths with wooden blades in their hands facing a squat, muscular man whose left eye was covered with a black patch. The short man was naked to the waist, and held a wooden sword in a hairy right hand. His voice was thickened by long years of quaffing the inferior wines of Urgal, and his face showed red in the sunlight.

Evmor was saying, "—pale pimps and sons of whores! I might as well try teaching the Naniko harlots to use a blade as you spineless spittles. Oh, come along. Line up and have at it again. I need a laugh to put me in a better humor."

Kothar cleared his throat. The squat man swung about, his one good eye taking in the muscular-bigness of the barbarian. He showed small teeth in a mirthless grin.

"What's this, another babe come to cut his teeth on a sword's edge? By the Kraken! I truly earn the little that Tor Domnus pays me."

Kothar rasped, "Save your breath, Evmor. I've killed better men than you with my bare hands. I'm here to wear the boar's head of Urgal on my jacket. Just show me where the armor is so I can go to work."

Evmor gaped. "So ho! A wit who can skip the training, he knows so much. He thinks that Evmor is

The man leaped, wooden blade slashing downward.

Kothar sprang inside the sweep of the blade. His left hand went up to catch Evmor's sword-wrist; his right fist slammed deep into the belly of the shorter man.

Evmor rocked back on his heels, waving his arms, mouths open and eyes bulging. He sat down abruptly on the courtyard cobbles and slid for three feet.

Evmor shook his head, then stared shrewdly up at Kothar.

"You may do, stranger. It's the first time that ruse has failed to work. You have good reactions, I'll say that. Do you know how to use that blade you carry as well as you do your fists?"

'Better." Evmor pulled himself to his feet by a hand on a weapon-rack. "Do you, now? Would you care to match me with the steel?"

The barbarian turned, yanked free a blade as long as his own, with a leather wrapping about the hilt, and tossed it at the squat man. Evmor caught it handily.

"Scratch me if you can," the barbarian grinned. Evmor flung himself at him. Kothar parried his blade with ease, for he had been schooled in use of the sword since childhood, first by his adoptive father—Kothar had never known his real father, nor his mother—and then by an old man-at-arms who had come back to Grondel Bay after a lifetime of serving the Southland kings as a warrior, who delighted in imparting all his weapon-wisdom to the boy Kothar.

"Three times Kothar parried before he struck back with the flat of the blade atop the skull, as he had done to Japthon. Evmor flung his arms wide, turned twice, witlessly, before he fell face down in the courtyard dust.

Kothar reached for a water-bucket, doused Evmor with its contents. Then he put a hand down and brought the man to his feet, where he swayed dizzily.

"No man's ever treated me so," Evmor complained ruefully, rubbing the top of his poll. His eyes watched the recruits gathered in a group, staring with big eyes and broad grins.

"Laugh now, you whore-sons," he growled. "This one's a man. You want me to turn him loose on you for weapon-play targets?"

He barked laughter when they shook their heads, their grins fading. Evmor put an arm about the barbarian. "You come with me, stranger. I want to talk to you about that trick you used just then, over a mug of ale in the buttery."

Kothar rumbled, "It was taught me by a man named Svairn. He fought much of his life in the Southlands."

"Did he now? Svairn of Grondel Bay? I knew him well. My treat for the ale, man of the north. Come along. You others—back to your wooden blades. And I hope you knock each others' skulls in."

Over their ale mugs, Evmor promised Kothar a jacket with the boar's head on it, and a shirt of mail to wear instead of his own. He vowed the barbarian he would be an officer in the riffraff Tor Domnus surrounded himself with, before the first fall winds came down from the hills.

Evmor complained about the recruits the prince of Urgal supplied him with, expecting him to make soldiers of them and the lack of honest fighting men in the army itself. He drank the strong ale with gusto, so much so that Kothar had to support him back to the little room that was his home in Urgal.

When the squat man invited him to share his comforts, Kothar nodded, loosed his mail shirt, casting it aside, and with Frostfire on the cot beside him, fell into a sound sleep. Time enough tomorrow, he told himself, to go hunting up the demon.

He woke to the smell of cooking meats and baking bread. Evmor was crouched at the brick hearth, busying himself with skillet and baking tins. When he saw Kothar yawn and toss his legs over the side of his cot, the squat man nodded:

"Food that sits well on an ale-tossed belly, this. Come and find a platter and heap it high. I eat best at an early hour, and enough to keep me going all the day."

"What about my uniform?" Kothar asked. He wanted battlement patrol duty. From the battlements where Athalia was said to walk, he could learn where Azthamur laired and visit him. He could not stroll about the battlements in his worn chain-mail shirt and bearskin cloak; he needed the disguise of the boar's head jacket.

Evmor waved a huge hand. "Later, later. Come and eat now, and tell me more of Svairn."

They feasted together, then Evmor took Kothar to the weapons room and fitted him out with a new chain-mail shirt and the leather jerkin with the insignia of Tor Domnus on it.

"You wear those well," commented Evmor. "I've lived my life as a fighting man. I was captain of the Foreign Guard for Queen Elfa of Commoral."

"Ah! Then you've good prospects for advancement here in Urgal. We've too few trained soldiers."

His duties on this first day were so light as to chafe the spirits of the big blond barbarian. He helped Evmor train the rookies, using a wooden sword, then polished his own weapons side by side with a couple of the castle guards. Kothar spoke little, except when spoken to; he used his ears to learn what he might of Azthamur.

During the conversation he swung the talk toward demons. "I sought employment by Candara of Kor, but I got into trouble during a fight at one of the taverns there. I made it out of the city two jumps ahead of her city guards."

A big Phalkaran chuckled. "Candara won't bother you much longer. Tor Domnus has plans for Kor."

"You make it sound as if I can expect good fighting. It's what I live for, a good fight."

"Her demoniac powers won't help her against Azthamur," grinned a scarred veteran of many wars. "We have our own demon, here in Urgal. He serves Tor Domnus well."

Kothar murmured, "Azthamur? I've never heard of that particular demon."

"You will if you stay here long enough."

"Azthamur lives in the caverns below the west battlement," muttered the veteran, making the sign of the ax that was the protective sign of Huldor, a beneficent demon who guarded innocent men and women from the wrath of other demons. "No one dares go there, excepting maybe Tor Domnus."

The west battlement. He was making progress, Kothar thought. He would ask Evmor for guard duty on that wall-walk during the night. He had no need to stay in Urgal long; his role of soldier under the boar's head banner was but a ruse. He lifted the shirt of chain-mail he had been polishing, studying it.

"Who guards the western bastion?" he asked casually.

The veteran hooted. "No need for a guard there, even if Evmor assigns one to the job. The demon patrols his own. No man would be fool enough to put his footprints there unless ordered to do so. Every so often Azthamur emerges and nobody ever sees the guard on duty again."

Better and better, the barbarian thought. This night I will walk those walks and go down the stairs to the lair where Azthamur guards the stolen god Xixthur. He felt tension creep into his muscles. Quite freely, Kothar would admit to a dislike for matching strengths with a demon, but it was his task to steal Xixthur, and this he meant to do.

Later, after the evening meal, he sought out Evmor.

"I am restless, friend. Give me a task to do that I may sleep better when I hit my pallet."

With a little persuasion, he got Evmor to agree to let him stand the watch. He ate early, of meat and bread and berry tarts, and when he moved up the narrow stone steps to the wall-walk, he felt strong and confident.

The night was cool, the winds over the Haunted Lands were blowing northward, carrying a dampness with them that chilled the bones in a man's body. Overhead the two moons of Yarth were bright silver against a dark sky in which thousands upon thousands of stars were visible. At one time, so the legends said, these stars were few and far between; now they were everywhere, like glistening pebbles on a beach.

Kothar paced up and down a few times, slowly. He carried the boar's head shield and the spear of the watchman, and Frostfire hung at his side. He must wait until the candle-lights, making the castle windows glow yellow in the night, were out before he dared leave his post and descend the narrow stairs.

It was as he was turning the corner to come back along the wall-walk that he saw her. She was standing, wrapped in a long cloak that hid everything but her white skull and the bones of her skeletal feet. She was staring at him with black, empty eye-sockets that were like pools of blackness, and when she moved, Kothar heard the grate of bones rubbing against bones.

"You came, Northman. Good!" she said.

"I wait for the castle to sleep."

"Pah! No need for that. Nobody dares come this way to see if you're on duty. The captain of the guards is a bloated thing, fat with rich foods and ale, who likes his comfort above all else."

Kothar moved to the narrow staircase door. The skeleton was there before him, in some eerie manner the barbarian could not explain; she seemed not to walk but rather to float.

"Let me go first, man from Cumberia. Azthamur knows me. I go often to bait him, to assure him that some day there will come one who will find a way to slay him."

"He does not harm you?"

"A demon like Azthamur cannot harm the dead." The door opened to her touch. Kothar watched her float through the opening with the short hairs on his neck standing stiffly. He liked not this consorting with a dead spirit, but Athalia was an ally of sorts, and he would accept her help if she chose to give it.

There were no torches on the stairs, only ebon blackness. But the bones of the skeleton gave off a subdued radiance by which Kothar could see to plant his feet. Down they went, ever downward, past the ground floor of the castle and into regions where a charnel smell added its odors to the mustiness of the air.

"By Dwalka! A man might rot here if he stayed very long. Get me out of this place, woman."

"Soon, Northman. Soon."

The stairs led down into water. The skeletal figure floated above those waters, but she assured Kothar that they were shallow, and he moved on catlike feet through the wetness until a low archway showed ahead. Now the stink was more noisome than ever, and the barbarian, who loved the clean air of mountainside and plain, came close to retching.

Here and there, Kothar could see human and animal bones scattered about indiscriminately. There were some bodies that still had flesh upon their bones, half eaten, rotting. Kothar cursed the demon beneath his breath.

"Aye, he is a curse on mankind," whispered the spirit woman. "He has lived so long in Urgal, feasting at first on human blood, that he has acquired a taste for flesh, which is why he sometimes goes out upon the wall-walk and devours a guard."

Kothar stepped under the archway, seeing a faint blue light coming from the walls. He was surprised, for the chamber before him was like a great room in the castle above, walled with woods of varying hues, with a rock ceiling overhead and a smooth floor underfoot.

A hundred chests and coffers stood about the room, thrust back against the wooden walls. Some of their lids were up, revealing ropes of pearls and golden urns, chalices and coins. He was a little dazzled by such wealth; demons had no need for riches.

"Of all the loot taken by Tor Domnus, a part is granted to the demon, who lends his help when the prince goes forth to rob a caravan. Tor Domnus, though very greedy, does not mind. Azthamur is his insurance against defeat. Besides, the loot never really leaves his castle, since the demon dwells here in its sub-cellars."

Kothar heard a footstep. His hand, went to his sword-hilt and very slowly, without noise, he drew Frostfire naked from its scabbard. He waited, listening to those footfalls. Beside him, the skeleton that had been the Princess Athalia did not stir.

The air in this cavern chamber was sweet, it had none of the charnal odor of the outer caves. A sweet wind swept through the room, carrying the salt scent of musk and incense. It was the lair of a sybarite and sensualist.

Then a woman stepped into the room.

CHAPTER THREE

She had been weeping, Kothar saw.

Her eyes were red, her smooth white cheeks, glistened with tears. She wore a white samite gown, rent down one side so that her pale thigh and hip showed through the opening. Her hair was long and brown, and her beauty was enough to make a man stare in awe.

"Philisia," breathed the skeleton.

The woman raised her face, stared through her tears at Kothar and the dead Athalia Her soft red mouth opened. She gasped.

"Are you victims of the demon, too?" she whimpered.

Kothar grunted, "I'm here to slay him." Philisia looked at Athalia "I have heard of you, dead one. Men say you prowl the battlements howling out your fury against Azthamur."

The skeleton was silent.

"Where is the demon?" asked Kothar.

"Coming, coming," whimpered the woman with the long brown hair. "He is going to eat me. Tor Domnus gave me to him. I—I was the prince's m-mistress. He tired of me and —"

She halted; whirled, putting a hand to her mouth. It sounded as if some great, scaled being was stepping on stones. Kothar tightened his grip on Frostfire. Then the thing was in the room and the barbarian stared at a monstrous thing that was a parody of humankind and—of a fish.

Glittering blue scales covered its body. Its mouth was huge, running the width of its fish-like features, set with double teeth at the top and bottom of its jaws. Its single eye was a brilliant blue and shone with evil laughter. Wide shoulders, also scaled, and long arms, with legs that bulged with muscles beneath the bluish-white scales, spoke of the raw power of this monster.

"What's this? Another victim for my appetite?"

"Not so, Azthamur!" cried the skeletal woman. "This is the man who has come to slay you, as I have promised many times."

The woman Philisia slipped past a small fire glowing in a ring of fire-stones, and moved to stand beside Kothar. "Save me, barbarian!" she breathed. "Save me and I belong to you."

Kothar grinned mirthlessly. He had no need of a woman at the moment, he was too concerned with staying alive while Azthamur died. The fish-like creature was advancing on him steadily, arms by its side. Apparently he was counting on the fear that usually paralyzed the guards on the wall-walks when he came for them, to keep Kothar helpless.

The barbarian heaved up Frostfire. The steel flashed in the bluish light as he drove its edge at the neck of the creature.

A man would have lost his head before that savage blow. Azthamur grunted and reeled backward, respect showing in his large blue eye. The demon showed no blood, nor was its scaled flesh marred by so much as a scratch. Azthamur shook himself, then sprang forward.

Kothar met him with the point of his sword. It did not wound the fish-man but it slowed him. The barbarian drove the hilt of his blade into the demon's face.

Then scaled arms were closing about him, lifting him off his feet. Kothar put the blade of his sword against the thickly thewed neck of the fish-man catching the flat of the blade in a hand. He pushed the edge of the sword against that thinly scaled throat with all his strength, until his back muscles were bulging out his chain-mail shirt.

"I'll break your back, man!" snarled Azthamur. "I'll leave you writhing helpless on the floor while I eat Philisia before your eyes— and when I'm hungry enough, I'll start on you."

"Foulness," grated Kothar, applying more pressure.

Slowly he was bending the fish-head backward. Azthamur was grimacing with the effort of fighting the steel blade across his throat. If the demon maintained the bear's hug of his long arms about the barbarian, then his neck would snap, sooner or later. Suddenly the thickly muscled arms loosened. Azthamur caught Kothar by a wrist, whirled him away. The Cumberian staggered, trying to regain his balance. Then the fish-man was upon him.

A scaled hand darted out, caught up the spear Kothar had dropped when Azthamur attacked. Spear held between his fingers, the demon leaped.

One single swing of Frostfire slashed the half of the spear. The point fell to clang on the stone floor. Yet the remnant of the long shaft rammed into the barbarian's belly, knocking him backward.

As he fell, Kothar slashed again with Frostfire, hitting the demon on the side of the head and knocking him into a coffer of rare black pearls from the depths of the Outer Sea. Azthamur, stumbled, fell over the chest and rolled along the floor.

The barbarian righted his big body, stood a moment on widespread legs. He saw the gills of the fish-man opening and closing, just below his rib case on either side of his scaled body. By Dwalka, but the monster knew it was in a fight!

Kothar leaped, sword-point aiming at that long blue eye.

The demon was faster, twisting away, his scaled hand stabbing for a curved scimitar from the Southlands, bringing it down with a flash of blue light on steel. The scimitar drove sideways, ringing against the long, straight blade of the magic sword.

Curved blade and straight glinted in the pale azure light as demon fought with man. Kothar set himself for a battle to the death, knowing the odds against him. Azthamur might slay him with the scimitar. No matter how often and how hard he struck the demon, even the blue steel of Frostfire seemed unable to cut the demon scales.

For long moments, they fought. Philisia stood with the skeleton woman, hands clasped before her, brown eyes glowing as they watched the play of the steel blades. The skeleton made no sound, it waited with rigid back and high-held head, staring with empty eye-sockets at that one-sided duel.

It was Philisia who whimpered, "Look! Azthamur drives him back. Turn, man—run if you can. No living thing can defeat Azthamur!"

Kothar did not hear her. His every sense was attuned only to the clanging contact of the blades. Never had he fought like this, never before had there been no chance at all of victory for his sword, no matter what the odds he faced.

Against Azthamur, he fought vainly and without hope. Steel could not kill this monster. Nothing could do that. Nothing! Yet he fought on, sullenly yielding ground. He would not turn his back and run, as Philisia counseled. He would fight until the scimitar came drinking of his life's blood, like the warrior he was.

41

Back, always backward, the demon pressed the man.

Now skeletal Athalia and the terrified Philisia were some distance away, and Kothar battled directly under the archway leading into the charnel caverns. Even his mighty muscles were tiring by this time, and Frostfire was a terrible weight in his right hand. It took more and more effort to swing his sword to meet the sweeping slashes of the scimitar.

"Rash human," panted Azthamur. "I'll enjoy eating you more than any meal I've ever tasted."

"Kill me first, before you gloat!" Kothar rasped. "The killing will come soon. You are beaten." The scimitar flashed and darted. It clanged against the hilt of the straight sword, it made Kothar skip and dance to its weaving patterns. Kothar told himself steel would never defeat Azthamur. There must be some other way.

He hurled his blade, leaped sideways. His hands went down, laid hold of a great rock tumbled among others on the cavern floor. His muscles creaked with strain but he got the rock up and above his head, and as the demon charged, he flung it.

The stone caught Azthamur on his scaled chest. Its sheer weight bowled him over so that he went backward to land on the stone floor with his spine. Before he could twist away, Kothar was on him.

A hand turned the demon. Kothar slid his forearms under the armpits of the fish-man. His hands met behind his neck, locked fingers. In this wrestling grip, he held the panting monster for a few seconds, bending his head forward with massive strength.

But Azthamur only laughed softly, half under his breath, and his demon muscles tightened and his arms came down against the arms of Kothar where the barbarian held him. Slowly, he broke that cunning grip, pressing down with his arms until Kothar grunted in the pain of the holding.

"Were I more demon now than man, you would have died in agony long ago," Azthamur rasped. "But I have put on human guise, and that weakens my demoniac powers—just enough so that you can put up a good fight against me."

"Enough that I can snap your neck!"

"Not so, man," panted Azthamur, and broke the hold of the gripping fingers at his throat.

Kothar rolled away, the demon turning to come after him.

The pale light from the inner chamber was almost no light at all in these outer caverns. There was a sheen on the shallow waters, glinting bluely where those reflections were, and its sight made Kothar realize suddenly that in that water, the demon would be much like the fish.

As Azthamur came for him, the barbarian lifted a rock in his hand and drove it sideways at the face before him. He had aimed for the blue eye, but the demon ducked slightly and took the stone across its temple. Momentarily stunned, it was no match for an aroused Kothar battling savagely for his life.

He whirled Azthamur, tripped him with a foot. They fell together into the shallow waters, and as that wetness closed about him, Kothar sought once again for a hold on the thick neck of the fish-man. His fingers tightened on scaly flesh, sank deep.

Grimly, Kothar hung to his clasp on that throat. Azthamur needed air for his lungs, having assumed quasi-humanoid shape. The only way for him to get that air was through his windpipe. But the demon was far too strong for the merely human hands that held him.

Azthamur reared up, dripping water, dragging Kothar with him, and his fists slammed hard into his belly. The barbarian grunted. Each blow was like that of a sledgehammer in the hands of a strong man. His finger-grip loosed, fell away.

He let go his hold with a quickness that surprised the fish-man. Kothar dropped backward and his mightily thewed legs came up to clamp about the demon's middle. Kothar heaved with all his body and Azthamur toppled forward into the water.

Like a cat, the barbarian shifted position. His legs inched higher, his hands stabbed toward the thick neck and tightened on the scaled flesh once again. With all his power, he held the fish-head below the surface of the rolling cave waters.

It was as the demon was bunching his back to throw him off that Kothar remembered a truth his adoptive father had told him once in a fishing smack out of Grondel Bay. A fish can drown in water, he had said. And Kothar blessed his memory as his legs inched further upward on that monstrous body until his thick thighs were clamped tight about the gills below the fish-man's rib case.

The demon gulped in air and water, his head still below the surface.

Not until his lungs were full of water that his gills could not pass out, did he realize the trick Kothar had played upon him.

Now indeed did his back arch and his muscles bulge as he fought desperately to free himself of that death-grip on his throat. But his lungs were taut with water, and he coughed fiercely underwater and every time he coughed, he swallowed more of the brackish liquid. Kothar kept his thighs clamped tight. His fingers were like stone as they sank deep into weakening throat muscles.

After a time, Azthamur quieted. But still the barbarian kept his grip. Not until the skeleton woman and Philisia came creeping through the cavern murk toward him did he realize that the demon might be dead. Slowly his fingers loosened; they ached with the strain of that terrible clasping. Azthamur never moved.

Kothar rose, to his feet, stood above the floating body. He panted and shivered in the aftermath of his battle. He reached down, caught the fish-body and yanked it upward onto the ooze-wet stones.

"Bind him," breathed the skeletal woman. "No need for that. He's dead."

"Bind him, just the same," she advised. Philisia ran with her hands filled with wire torn from a hanging ornament, and with this, Kothar knelt and bound the demon. When he was done, he stood and stared at Athalia and at the woman with the long brown hair who shivered in her torn court gown.

"Xixthur," Kothar said. "I must find him." The skeletal woman went and sat on a flat rock, knees together, bony jaw resting on equally bony knees, and she stared down at the motionless Azthamur with empty eye-sockets. The woman of flesh and blood crept closer to the barbarian and plucked at his fur cloak.

"Xixthur is not in the caves of Azthamur," she breathed.

The barbarian whirled on her. "What's this? Are you telling me I'm here on a fool's errand?"

She smiled and shook her head. She was not as young a woman as he had thought from his first glimpse of her, Kothar realized; yet neither was she old. There were tiny lines at the corners of her eyes and a bitterness to the quirk of her lips that marked her as a woman who had seen sin and suffering, and was not untouched by them.

Her body was heavily curved, almost overripe with wanton fleshiness. The brown hair had come loose in the jeweled fastenings that had held it; it was this that made her seem younger. Parts of her gown were torn here and there so that the pale tints of her flesh gleamed in the rents.

"Where is Xixthur, then?" he asked. "In the apartments of Kylwyrren, the magician who serves Tor Domnus."

Kothar picked up Frostfire from the floor where it had fallen in the fight and slid the blue blade back into its scabbard. "Then I will find Kylwyrren and take it away from him."

Her smile was patient. "You would have to fight your way through half of Tor Domnus's soldiers, man. I know a better way, up the hidden stairways that only I, of all the people in Urgal am well aware of."

Kothar caught her arm. "Then lead the way, woman."

He turned to stare back at Athalia, crouched above the motionless form of Azthamur. Well, her vengeance for the long-ago death of her lover was an accomplished thing, now. He would leave her here to gloat and enjoy her triumph.

Philisia walked ahead of him with sure steps, across the smooth stone floor of this chamber that had belonged to Azthamur and, parting a hanging drapery, slipped through and up a flight of narrow stone steps. Kothar followed on her heels.

"Why do you alone know this way?" he wondered.

"My father was castellan for Tor Domnus, before Tor Domnus saw my beauty and took me into his bed." Philisia sighed. "My father objected, he did not want his daughter to be any man's mistress, even to a prince. Tor Domnus ordered my father slain."

She sighed. "Since then, I have hated the prince of Urgal, though I have continued to be his harlot. Until some nights ago when a trader out of Zoane in Sybaros carried in to him a blonde woman who caught Tor Domnus's eye and roused his passions.

"Tor Domnus bought the woman.

"Me, he gave this night to the demon." She turned and flashed a smile back at him. "You saved me from Azthamur, barbarian. Now I belong to you."

45

Kothar growled, "I have no need for a woman, Philisia. My errand for Queen Candara demands that I travel alone."

"You will not leave me here to be ravished by the soldiery? Or tortured to death to amuse Tor Domnus's new bed-mate?"

The Cumberian rasped a curse. "You'll have to keep up with me. I must flee like the wind once I lay hands on Xixthur."

"I will ride with you, as fast or as slowly as you like. I am not a weak woman." She slowed her upward progress, cautioning him with a waving hand. "Hush now. We approach the apartments where Kylwyrren dwells."

They were in utter darkness. They stood on a flat landing so close that the barbarian could feel the soft body of the woman against his own. He felt her tremble, he put his thickly muscled arm about her slim middle, drew her closer to give her added courage.

Her warm hand pressed his. Then she was slipping from his grasp and fumbling in the ebon blackness. A narrow panel slid back, revealing the back of a brocade hanging. She breathed into his ear, "This is a wall in the apartments of the mage. Step carefully, and make no sound."

She thrust aside the drapery and Kothar followed her into a stone chamber filled along its walls with shelves and cabinets that held the assorted impedimenta of a magician. Curious glass vials and Oddly shaped urns and jars contained the magical properties with which Kylwyrren worked his spells.

The chamber was lighted by a reflection from a lamp in another room. Philisia held her forefinger to her lips, then beckoned him. As noiselessly as a cat, Kothar went after her.

They paused before a round tower room, where a single lamp shed its radiance upon a squat metal thing, with eyes of glass here and there in its rounded bulk, which rested on three thin metal legs. It stood about two feet in height and was, perhaps, the ugliest thing that Kothar had ever seen.

His eyes went to a cadaverous man with dank black hair, clad in a robe embellished with silver threadings woven with the names of the thousand and three demons known to man. His elbows rested on his knees, his dark eyes, brooded on the metal object perched before him.

The barbarian scanned the mage more closely. There was no sign of a weapon close to the magician, nor did it seem that he could have a dagger hidden beneath his robes. Kothar drew a deep breath.

Kylwyrren must have heard him, for he turned and his bold eyes stared out from under tufted eyebrows at the man and woman, Philisia gave a little cry.

Kylwyrren said softly, "I would never have believed it."

Philisia cried, "Tor Domnus gave me to Azthamur this night, Kylwyrren. This man from Cumberia saved my life."

It was as if the magician had not heard her. "For ages, there have been legends. To our people, they were only that, like fairy tales made to interest little children. But—here before me is the proof."

He swung back to the metal thing, slapped his hand against it. "The legends say that once the race, of men went to the stars, all the stars and to the planets around them. That once our universe was an expanding one, that the suns were flung outward into space by a single titanic blast of matter.

"Now the universe is old. Old!

"The star-suns are falling back upon themselves, back to that beginning of all Time and all Space. When they come together in a fantastic crash and gathering—together of all Matter—will the process begin all over again?"

Kothar listened without understanding. He knew the ways of a sword in his hand and the fury of a battle, the cry of the wolves along the frozen barrens of his homeland, but he knew nothing of stars and planets. His feet had burned in the desert sands, he was familiar with habits of hawk and eagle, deer and horse, but such things as Time and Space and Matter were unknown to him,

He rasped, "Is that Xixthur?"

The magician smiled in his bemusement. "Aye! This is Candara's god, this gross thing of glass and metal. Early men made this, barbarian. Early men, with a knowledge of matter that no man today knows anything of. Even my magic might be weak beside their wisdom. I could never make such a thing as this."

Philisia forgot her uneasiness to ask, "What is it?"

"Candara calls it a god. In a sense, I suppose it is. But I have read

47

old manuscripts, ancient parchments that tell the legends of early men, and I know that it is a thing that gives off what early man called "rays."

"These rays destroyed sick tissue in a human body, they killed germs, they repaired flesh and bone and muscle. Don't ask me how. They did. I have not those ancient wisdoms. No wonder Candara grieves to lose it! No wonder she wants it back. This thing will give her eternal youth."

"Eternal youth?" Philisia quavered, coming a step closer. "Will it give that to me too, Kylwyrren?"

"Assuredly. You see this tiny bit of metal? You move it so—"

Kothar saw the glass eyes in the metal hull glow with light, and heard the faint hum of the thing. The radiance from the eyes went everywhere, forming a kaleidoscope of red and blue and yellow throughout the chamber.

"—and somehow," continued Kylwyrren," the rays given off by this Xixthur repairs the ills of the human body and reinvigorates it, giving it strength and youth. I do not know whether it would make an old person young—my knowledge extends only so far—but I am positive it will keep a man or woman from aging any more."

Philisia exclaimed, "Ohhh!"

Kothar moved forward, his hand on his sword-hilt. "I must take it away from you, magician. It belongs to Candara. She has sent me for it, to fetch it back to her."

The magician nodded. "I expected some such attempt. So also does Tor Domnus. I am alone at the moment, but his soldiers patrol the halls and corridors. You can never hope to get away with it."

"I must try." The woman said softly, "He must bind and gag you, old man. We do not dare permit you to give the alarm."

Kylwyrren nodded, sighing. "Yes, you must do that. I have served Tor Domnus for many years, but he is a hard taskmaster and I have no love for him. Why should I risk cold steel in my flesh?"

He stood up and turned, putting his skinny arms behind his back for their tying. Kothar made short work of the task, he caught the man and lowered him to the floor, and there he bound his ankles. Philisia placed a cloth between his teeth and her slender white fingers knotted the thong that held it in place.

In a moment, the barbarian had swept up Xixthur into the crook of an arm and turned to follow Philisia through the secret panel of the hidden doorway. She stood beside the drapery, half lifting it.

It was then that the arched door at the other end of the tower chamber opened. Alma came into the room, calling out the name of Kylwyrren. He was tall and broad of shoulder, with a hard face burned by desert sun and mountain wind. He wore a black velvet upon, and one black and one white velvet stocking on each leg. A dagger with a golden pommel hung by his hip."

Kothar was across the room, the weight of Xixthur like cotton batting to his muscles. His fist swept up and around. It landed on the astounded face of the startled man and drove him backward through the doorway and out into the tower corridor.

The barbarian slammed the arched door shut, dropped a metal bar across two slots on either side. "That will keep them busy for a while, trying to breakdown the door."

He ran for the hidden panel where Philisia stood, half-swooning in her terror. "That was Tor Domnus himself you hit," she whimpered. "He will have us flayed alive for that!"

"Then run," growled Kothar, catching her by a shoulder and whirling her around, pushing her through the narrow panel.

He went after her, waited while she closed the panel. Then she was before him, shivering and moaning in her fear, until his hand caught her shoulder and his fingers tightened. "Don't be afraid," he breathed. She went more surely down the stone stairs and along the floor of the chamber of the demon Azthamur. The skeletal woman was still sitting beside the unloving body of the fish-man and did not turn her head as they ran past.

"Where to now?" rasped the barbarian. "We can't go up the stairs to the wall-walk. Tor Domnus has seen my face, knows I'm wearing his boar's head uniform."

Philisia shrank against him, shuddering. His arm went around her shoulders protectively. "I d-don't know," she told him.

"Think! The demon must come and go a secret way. He would not show himself in the streets of Urgal, would he—when Tor Domnus sends him on an eerie errand?"

"No-no. He is never seen by the common people."

He watched her thin brows settle into a thoughtful frown. Her tiny teeth nibbled at her lower lip and from time to time she sighed. Finally she shook her head.

"I'm sorry. I don't remember any hidden way down this far in the caverns."

Kothar stared around him at the wet stones and the shallow waters. He knew with that barbaric instinct that was so much a part of him that Azthamur came and went by secret ways to the castle and to Urgal. His stare was caught and held by the brackish water about his knees.

Azthamur was—or had been—a fish-man. What more likely means to travel in and out of his lair than by a water route? Somewhere in this cavern must be a subterranean stream that would carry Philisia and him safely out of Urgal.

He began to pad back and forth in the little pool, explaining his actions to the woman, who nodded her understanding. Holding her gown hip-high, she walked where he did not, slowly and with searching feet. Each of them knew that Tor Domnus was a raging maniac high above their heads, seeking entry into the tower rooms of Kylwyrren.

Yet the secret waterway eluded their eyes and their feet as they went from one end of the caves to the other. By now the prince of Urgal would be inside the tower, would have freed Kylwyrren and listened to his tale. Soldiers wearing the boar's head uniform of Tor Domnus would soon be flooding these lower cellars.

And then Philisia went out of sight.

CHAPTER FOUR

One moment, she was walking and the next she was sinking down into the water, crying out sharply. Kothar waded toward her, reached down, caught her by the hand, and yanked her up. She dripped wetly, her gown was plastered to her body but she laughed happily.

"It's there, some sort of hole, an opening in the rock. I went down into it. But—but it's dark down there."

"I'll go. You stay here. If it leads me beyond Urgal, I'll come back for you."

They heard the sound of footsteps on the distant stone staircase. Philisia shook her head. "No time for that. We go together. I'm not staying here to be caught by Tor Domnus's soldiers.

Kothar nodded. Shifting his grip on Xixthur, he stepped forward and sank downward like a stone, vaguely aware that the woman was following after him. For fifteen-feet he went straight-down, then saw dim light through the water ahead. He swam as best he could with the great weight of the metal god in his arms, but the water shallowed ahead and he was soon standing up to his middle thighs in water, inside a huge stones walled sea cave. Philisia gripped his sword-belt, yanked herself to her feet beside him.

"Where are we?" he wondered. "Somewhere on the shoreline of Urgon-lake, where there are many cliffs." She put her head to one side, gathering her brown hair in her hands and wringing out the droplets of water. "The lake is bordered by cliffs. This cave must be inside one of them, completely hidden from view."

"There's an opening of sorts up ahead. Come on." They waded across the cave to a strip of pale water lightened by shafts of moonlight. Kothar put Xixthur down on a stone ledge and dove. He came up in lake water with the moon low in the sky and a gigantic stone cliff rising behind him. He went back for Xixthur, and told Philisia what he had seen. She nodded, "Yes, the face of the cliff must reach underwater a few feet, just enough to hide the entrance into this cave. This is the path by which Azthamur came and went. It will serve to—let us get away."

She bent, tore the long sodden skirt of her gown until she was naked below her upper thighs. Her brown eyes flashed at him. "It makes swimming easier, with less of this thing to encumber me." Then she turned in the water and dove. They came up alongside the cliff face, kicking to buoy themselves in the deeper water. Xixthur was so heavy, Kothar was forced to grip a jutting section of rock to keep his head in the air.

"Certainly I can't swim with this thing," he growled. His eyes raked the sheer face of the cliff. "And that bluff doesn't afford any hand grips or toeholds to let me climb it."

He began to inch his way along the base of the cliff, holding Xixthur under an arm and using his free hand to find and cling to jutting parts of the cliff. A cool wind was blowing across the lake, from the forest on the other side. It was a lonely, desolate spot, considering the fact that it was so close to the city of Urgal, which raised its walls on the other side of the cliff.

"If Azthamur used the lake for his comings and goings," panted Philisia, "no man or woman in the city would use it. Perhaps, long ago, they did come here to swim—until the demon caught and ate a few."

"It helps us, that fact," Kothar admitted.

He found a narrow trail where the cliff-side ended, and lifted out of the water, putting the ray-machine on the ground and turning to lend a hand to Philisia, She sank down on solid ground at his feet, shivering. The water had been icy cold, the wind from the forests just as chilling. The myriad stars in the sky were fading from view before the first shafts of red sunlight coming from beyond distant Sybaros, which beached upon the salt waters of the Outer Sea.

"Let me rest," she begged. "There's no time for that. This early hour of the morning is the best time to travel, for there won't be many folk about to see and report us to Tor Domnus."

He bent, caught her hand, yanked her to her feet. She shivered, wet and miserable, against him. Kothar grinned, slapped her haunch.

"The sun will dry you off in the barrens between Urgal and Kor. But first we've got to find a stable and steal two horses."

She nodded, sniffling. "Tor Domnus keeps horses not far from here that are used by his couriers to travel with messages to the lords of Phalkar and Sybaros."

Kothar heaved Xixthur to a shoulder and planted his feet where Philisia walked. She went sure footedly through these woods, and there was an aliveness about her that made the barbarian realize that, for the first time in her life, she felt truly free. From time to time, she turned to flash a smile at him.

She slowed her steps as they came to the edge of the woods that bordered on a wide-road running between Urgal and Phalkar to the north. As he stood within the leafy boskage of leaves and bushes, Kothar could make out the big barns and stables, he caught the smell of horseflesh, he heard a man rattling tools about inside a large shed.

"There will be guards here and there," she whispered.

The barbarian grunted. Alone and without Xixthur, he might have risked as direct attack, simply going into the stables, snatching a horse and galloping off. With Philisia to consider, he must use caution.

He said, "There's a low roof there," nodding at a thatched section of the stable roof. "I'm going up to have a look."

He was catlike in his leap to the eaves, swinging up easily, with a bunching of muscles-beneath his tanned hide. Then he was moving over the stable roof to another roof and down that until the watching woman lost sight of him.

His eyes took in the big yard, the troughs, the bales of hay piled close to the wall of the big barn. The sunlight was a hot warmth bathing fences and well-stones with the buckets resting on their cappings. The heat of this early morning sun drew the sweat from a man and caused heat waves to dance across the distant desert.

His hand touched the thatching of the roof, brushed over it. It had been baked by that hot sunlight until it crackled with dryness. Thatch would burn like tinder, he thought, as would the bales of hay just below his perch on the roof. Kothar grinned and his fingers went hunting in his belt-purse for steel and flint.

He crouched, struck a spark, another spark, then blew as it caught fire. He made a hasty torch of the thatch-work and, waving it above his head to make that fire blaze, he tossed it downward.

An instant later a thin thread of gray smoke was rising upward from the hay. Kothar turned and scrambled across the rooftop to the low edge, from which he leaped. He ran to find Philisia hidden in some berry bushes.

"I'll fetch three horses," he told her. "Be ready to mount."

He whirled and ran. By this time a stable-hand had seen the smoke, had sensed the gathering flames inside the hay. His hoarse shouts brought men and boys at the run.

Their first concern was the horses. They ran inside the stables, drove out every mount. Kothar watched those horses run, his eyes taking in their legs, their glossy coats, the depth of their barrels. He selected a big roan for himself, a smaller mare for Philisia. He needed a third horse to carry Xixthur; he would use reins or straps to fasten it on.

He was up and running, bent over. His hands went to the reddish mane of the big, rangy roan; an instant later his leg was swinging over his back and he thumped down onto its bare back. The roan wore no bridle but the mare did, and so did the heavyset brown stallion he had chosen to carry Xixthur.

The men and boys were too busy inside the stables and the barns to notice him as he galloped off with the mare and the brown behind him. Only when he paused to snatch up a fallen bridle did a youngster see him and open his mouth to yell a warning.

Kothar leaped. The back of his hand took the youth across the jaw, toppled him backward into a water trough. The boy would recover soon enough, and yell the warning, but Kothar had had some few precious minutes in which to seat Philisia and fasten Xixthur on the brown horse.

The woman came at the run, bare white legs below her torn gown flashing whitely in the sunlight. She let Kothar throw her upward onto the mare; she caught the reins expertly; she was a good horsewoman, he saw. Then she called out instructions to Kothar as to how to lash the metal object inside a fold of the stolen reins. When it was done, the barbarian tested the tightened knots and nodded. Xixthur should stay put, no matter how fast the brown horse had to gallop.

He swung up onto the roan. An instant later they were pounding out across the fields east of the stables, heading toward the edge of the farm fields and beyond them, the desert.

They rode swiftly, but not at any killing pace. It would take time for the stable hands to alert the soldiers of Tor Domnus that the man they hunted was mounted now and on his way into the desert. By that time, they should be far ahead.

Past farmhouses and hay ricks they rode, and through fields furrowed to a nicety by a plow. While they cantered through an orchard, Kothar pulled down as many apples, as he could reach and stuffed them inside his boar's head leather jerkin. They would need food until they reached the ruined chapel where he had left Greyling and his weapons.

It was past noon when they came to the vast stretch of rock and sand that was the rim of the Barren Desert. Ahead lay a sea of sand and a few rocks, baking in the hot sunlight.

Philisia shivered and made a soft, whimpering sound, seeing all that desert lying before her. "I'll cook to death," she breathed, indicating the scantiness of her gown. Its low collar revealed her shoulders, white and smooth, its thinness emphasized the thrust of her breasts, the slenderness of her waist. Where she had torn its skirt, her legs showed pale almost to her hips.

Kothar barked, "Would you stay behind?" She bit her lower lip, shook her head. Then they were cantering out across the pebbles, seeking to conserve their strength and that of their horses. It was a long pull to Kor from Urgal; the way was broken only by the ruins of the ancient chapel where the barbarian had left Greyling. With the instinct of those who live their years in the wild, he guided the roan toward those ruins.

The blinding sunlight baked them. Sweat ran down their backs and along their faces. Kothar felt the bite of thirst and glanced at Philisia, seeing how she suffered. By Salara! Her skin would be burned red by nightfall! He yanked free his bearskin cloak, and with rough grace tossed it about her near nakedness.

She flashed him a weak, grateful glance. They rode on through the heat. Toward noon, Philisia moaned and swayed on her horse. The Cumberian urged the roan closer, reached out, gathered the girl up in a thickly thewed arm.

"You'll be easier, this way," he told her.

She cuddled against his chest, though the hot steel of his chain-mail shirt was like fire to her skin. She pillowed her head on his chest and let her body go limp. In moments she was asleep, utterly exhausted.

Staring straight ahead, bringing the mare and the brown horse behind him at the length of their tethers, he rode onward.

Instinct made him turn when he did to survey their back trail. His keen eyes made out four dots, far away. Kothar scowled, remembering that Tor Domnus kept fast horses for his couriers in those royal stables. The men following him would be riding the fastest horses the prince of Urgal owned.

He kicked the roan to a gallop from its slow canter. There was distance between himself and the men who followed and he wanted to maintain that distance as best he could.

He was many miles from the ruined chapel. His horn bow and long war-arrows in their quiver were at the chapel with Greyling. Until he held his horn bow in his hand, he would have no defense against those oncoming riders, other than his sword.

Grimly, Kothar stared straight ahead. The soft soughing of the sand under hoof, the hot wind burning his cheeks, the constant burning of the sun on his body, were the only indications the Cumberian had that he was trapped inside a nightmare. The weight of the sleeping girl in his arms was another guidepost to reality, as was the gnawing worry in his brain.

Those riders behind him would be coming fast. Faster than he dared drive the, roan and the other horses. They might overtake him before he came to the chapel. Then they could stand off at a distance and pick off the horses with arrows, and then feather their shafts in his chest.

He rode facing forward until he could hold back no longer. Then he swung about in the saddle and stared at the four men who were behind him.

"By Dwalka," he growled. They were almost within bow shot range. One of them, probably the best archer, was bringing his bow off his shoulder and reaching for an arrow with a hand. First shot for the brown horse, with Xixthur on it. Xixthur was more important than the man or the woman.

After that . . .

2.

Mindos Omthol was weeping softly in chagrin.

"So near, so near! Another few miles and he would be at the ancient

56

chapel of Randolphus. Then with his bow he could stand off those men, maybe slay them so he could get away."

The demon Abathon snorted.

"You are a fool, magician," he snapped. "You pride yourself on being able to make magic. Well, make a spell to aid him. It's that simple."

Mindos Omthol stared at the creature he had summoned up. He shook his head, muttering, "I am a fool, indeed. But you said yourself that I could not steal from a demon and—"

"Kothar has done your stealing for you; mage. No need to try and take Xixthur from him. In time, he will bring that metal thing to you, I believe. But right now, he needs a helping hand. Look!"

Mindos Omthol craned his leathery neck, saw the mailed chest of the barbarian and the woman who slept nestled within his arm. As he watched, an arrow-shaft flew overhead, winking brightly in the desert sunlight.

"A helping hand, yes. But I must not reveal to anyone that I've had a hand in it. I don't want Tor Domnus nor Queen Candara to come seeking me."

Abathon asked, "How about a rainstorm?" The magician took thought, finally nodding. "Yes. A heavy storm with rain like a cloudburst that will hide man and woman and horses from those who pursue."

He turned to his vials and alembics resting on a nearby tabletop. His big-veined hands darted out, closed on glass and marble. From each he poured noisome liquids into a chalcedony bowl, and into the pool of wetness he dropped pinches of ground wort-bane and hazel roots. Steam rose upward from the crucible.

Mindos Omthol began to chant. . . .

3.

The black cloud was on the horizon to the south. It came fast, and as it came, it spread out, and now Kothar could hear the rumble of distant thunder and see the flash of lightning inside that moving darkness. He had no suspicion of wizardry in the sight. Storms had been known before over desert lands. It was only the timing of the approaching storm that made him wonder.

An arrow missed the brown horse. "By Dwalka," snarled the barbarian, kicking the roan to a faster pace "if that cloud brings rain to hide us, we may still make it."

The cloud was overhead. It came to a stop. Those black, fluffy masses opened up and water came down. Like a flood in spate was that water, that drenched man and woman and beast, until it grew hard to breathe.

Kothar turned the roan aside, angled its walk in a slightly different direction. Now if those riders should gallop forward, blind in this drenching downpour, they would never be able to find them.

The rain woke Philisia. She lifted her head, letting the cool moisture drench her skin and hair and the thin stuff of her torn gown until the samite was plastered to her generous curves.

"Do I dream?" she asked.

"If you do, I dream myself. It's rain, right enough. And it couldn't have come at a better time."

Her laughter rang out. "I'm cool again, and not thirsty any more." She opened her red mouth and let the water drops beat down inside her throat, swallowing greedily from moment to moment.

The horses moved at a walk, now that there was no immediate reason for haste. In such a downpour, Kothar could not see the ruined chapel until he was upon it, he knew. But as long-as the rain continued, he was safe, and it showed no sign of stopping.

All he had to guide him now was his instinct. He remembered where the chapel was, and his knees turned the roan in that direction. Greyling had been too well trained to whinny at approaching horses, and so he knew he could not count on guidance from his warhorse. He did not want his own mounts to whinny for fear they might attract the attention of the four men who pursued them.

It was an eternity in the downpour, with all that wet grayness deluging the desert around them, making tiny pools where the stones and pebbles were clustered. The horses plodded, splashing through those pools, shaking their heads and blowing their delight in the cool wetness, that steamed on their hides.

The graystone arch loomed black in the rain, and beside it the crumbling wall of what had been a monastery showed long and low. Kothar grinned his pleasure through tight lips.

"He urged the roan toward the tiny roof of the old shed where he had stored his weapons and left Greyling. As the roan neared the fallen timbers, Kothar heard a faint nicker. He let his laughter out softly, below his breath.

Then he was lowering Philisia to the ground and swinging down, finding Greyling at his elbow, bumping his back with his Roman nose, in affectionate greeting. Kothar rubbed fingers along the gray nose, whispered words into the silky gray ears.

Philisia murmured, "This is Randolphus's chapel. I saw it once, long ago, in a picture book. What are we doing here?"

"Recovering my weapons," the Cumberian grinned.

He moved to a wrapping and unrolled it, disclosing the horn-bow that he had from old Pahk Mah when he had rescued his daughter. He bent the bow, fitted the string to it. Then he set the bow and his quiver of war-arrows against a well-wall protected from the rain by the leaded-roof.

"If those men find us now, I'm not completely helpless. I, too, can fire war-arrows—and I'm a better shot than that lout who was shooting at our horses."

She crowded against him, shivering, seeking warmth and courage from his nearness. This huge barbarian was like a rock pillar to Philisia. His keen wits and bulging muscles had delivered her from dreaded Azthamur, he had brought her safely out of Tor Domnus's castle with the metal object which Candara called a god. He had, by some trick she could not understand, made it rain, and then had found shelter here in this old chapel.

Philisia was grateful. She slipped her bare arms upward about his neck, dragged his mouth down to her soft lips. They clung together in their kiss for long moments.

Then Kothar growled, "We have no time for foolishness, girl. Much as I'd enjoy bedding you down, that is. First, we'll ride to Kor and then we'll beg a bed of Candara where we can frolic as we will."

She sighed and nodded, nestling her head to his chest but still clinging to his neck with her arms. "You are my lord, Kothar. I'll go and do whatever you say."

Kothar wondered if the prohibition Afgorkon had laid on him extended to women. This Philisia was a treasure of sorts, but as long as he carried Frostfire by his side, he could own no treasure. He sighed. He would have to wait and see, where Philisia was concerned.

The rain was letting up.

He could see a hundred yards from the chapel now, and soon, almost to the horizon. A faint white mist clung to the ground where the rain made steam on the hot desert sands. That mist would be almost as good as rain in hiding them from the four warriors who wore the boar's head device.

From a saddlebag on Greyling's saddle, he drew out cold meat and bread and a flagon of cool water. Philisia seated herself on a stone bench and munched happily, eyes glowing as they studied the graceful bulk of the Cumberian moving to and fro, preparing for their departure.

"It will be night, soon. That rain lasted all afternoon. Our horses' hoofs will make little sound on the desert sands. By dawn, if we ride all night, we ought to be in Kor."

When the meat and bread were gone and the flagon empty, Kothar rose to his feet and stretched out a hand to the girl. Overhead the stars were appearing, scattered across the blue sky with a myriad generosity that made the evening heavens brilliant above them.

"There'll be moonlight too, but the moons of Yarth don't show the desert as clearly as does the sun. I think we'll be all right."

The barbarian mounted on Greyling, he helped Philisia up on her mare. He reached for the reins to draw the brown horse after them, letting the roan trail free.

He turned the gray toward Kor.

4.

And in the city of Kor, Queen Candara brooded.

60

She sat cross-legged on a stool in the necromancer chamber of hunchbacked Zordanor watching the misshapen man as he peered into a bowl of molten silver where gleamed the night stars and the two moons of Yarth and the vast stretches of the Barren Desert.

Candara rested her dimpled chin on a fist, while her black eyes seemed to stare at far-off visions. Truly, she had never really expected the barbarian to steal Xixthur from the demon Azthamur. She had been hopeful, yes; she had counted on the magicks of the mage Zordanor, who had predicted success; yet in her heart, since she knew the strength and wicked wiles of Azthamur, she had resigned herself to defeat and the resultant aging process which would, in time, turn her into an old woman.

"What do I do with him now?" she asked querulously.

Zordanor waved an impatient hand, gesturing her to silence. "They come, the barbarian and the prince's former mistress. They will be before the city gate by sunrise. The four men who trailed them have turned back to meet Tor Domnus and the soldiers he is bringing with him."

Candara straightened. Her fist hit her thigh angrily. "To wage war with me? He would dare?"

"Who can read the mind of a man like Tor Domnus? Not I, nor any magician alive. But if Tor Domnus knows the value of Xixthur, as I am sure he must—since Azthamur will have told him of its value— then I feel confident he will hurl his soldiery at your walls, to secure the metal god for his own use."

"I must prevent him, Zordanor I am not so strong in Kor, as I would like, and the loyalty of my hired mercenaries is a chancy thing, at best."

The hunchback nodded. "Aye. But how?" Candara tossed her foot as her brows furrowed. She was not often given to thought, she cared more for the carnal pleasures of the flesh than the cerebral enjoyments of the mind. Yet her mind was good. She was no fool, for all her follies, and when she reasoned, she thought much as a man will think.

"I need help, Zordanor. Greater help than you can give."

His ugly face showed surprise. "And who in these Haunted Lands can give you aid that is beyond my powers?"

"Mindos Omthol, the necromancer."

The misshapen man gasped. His eyes narrowed and his nostrils flared to his breathing. He swayed back and forth, oddly toad-like, but his huge head nodded slowly.

The old mage lived in a remote corner of the Haunted Lands, beside the Sunken Sea bottom out of which the first life on Yarth was said to have crawled eons ago, in a gaunt black tower filled with the secrets of necromancy and old wizardry. No man traveled near the black tower, for an certain nights hellish fires could be glimpsed from its narrow windows and more than one traveler told of screams of fear and agony resounding from its walls.

It was common knowledge in the Haunted Lands that Mindos Omthol knew all there was to know of arcane wisdom. His vials contained elixirs, and nostrums, lenitives and concoctions which had no like anywhere in the lands between the Salt Ocean and the Outer Seas. With such materia medica, the old Image could perform any incantation.

"Certainly he knows more than I," muttered Zordanor, "and far more than Kylwyrren who serves Prince Tor Domnus."

"You approve my choice, then?"

"I do—under the circumstances. Mindos Omthol can summon up demons from the lowest tiers of the nether worlds. Awful demons." Zordanor shuddered. "But he demands a high price for his enchantments. A price you may not be willing to pay."

Candara made a grimace. "It is pay his price—or that of Tor Domnus. I would rather trust the old man than the young."

She stood, regal in a black gown that clung faithfully to her splendid body. "You shall accompany me, Zordanor. You and Mindos Omthol can make wizard talk together. Perhaps you can make him name a sensible price for his labors."

The hunchback shook his head dubiously, "Mindos Omthol cannot be swayed by words. But we shall see."

Within the hour two fast horses were saddled and bridled at the postern gate of the castle, that faced the more desolate areas of the Haunted Lands. Zordanor came first, peering quickly with his eyes, then swinging his neck about so he could see Queen Candara, wrapped in a black wool robe, descend the two stone steps and place a sandaled foot in the ivory stirrup of her saddle.

Moments later, they galloped out across the wastes.

They rode swiftly, for Zordanor had prepared certain spells that shrank the land beneath their horses' hoofs. Before noon, they were reining-up before the red metal door set in the black stone wall of the ancient tower.

"Who comes before Mindos Omthol?" boomed a voice.

"Queen Candara of Kor," answered Zordanor, "together with her court magician. We would ask help of Mindos Omthol against our mutual enemy."

"Mindos Omthol has no enemies."

"I speak of Tor Domnus of Urgal."

"There was a little silence. Then the red door slid back and a brass man moved from its shadows, clanking out onto the rocky ground surrounding the tower. The metal giant made a bow and its voice boomed out like thunder muffled in a narrow gorge.

"Mindos Omthol will see you. Follow me."

Candara slipped from the saddle and walked with Zordanor across the pebbles toward the opening of the red door. Inside herself, she was frightened. She knew the powers of a mage like Mindos Omthol, she understood that by coming to see him to beg his help she well might be placing herself within his necromantic powers.

She told herself she had no choice. Well enough she knew that Tor Domnus would follow Kothar to the gates of Kor and inside them, to wrest Xixthur from his grasp. And Candara could not give up Xixthur! She would die, were she to do that. And the queen of Kor found life very sweet and satisfying to her senses.

Inside the black tower it was cool, the air was scented sweetly; by magic, she was sure. Ahead of her, the metallic man clanked up the narrow stone staircase. Slightly below her came Zordanor who was no match for Mindos Omthol in the casting of spells and wizardries. She had poor weapons to serve her, she told herself.

The brass man halted on a little landing. Its gleaming arm drew back certain draperies and Candara stepped forward into a round chamber with stone walls covered with cabinets holding any number of necromantic volumes and vials, alembics and philtre pots.

The mage himself stood grim and tall beside a golden pillar that supported a large crystal ball. He was poised within the red lines of a pentagram, at which sight Zordanor gasped and shrank back, for no magician stood inside the pentagram unless he summoned evil demons.

"Be not afraid," Mindos Omthol cried. "I have sent the demon Abathon back into his own hells. I am alone."

As if to display the truth of his assertion, he stepped over the red pentagram on the floor and advanced upon Queen Candara. His old eyes glowed at sight of her sultry beauty, for upon entering the room the queen had slipped back the hood of her robe.

She held out her hands. The magician caught them in his own, bent and kissed each one.

"I am here to serve you, highness," he murmured. Candara admitted surprise. This old man was courtly, polite, vastly different from most of the mages she had known in her lifetime. There was none of the arrogance of someone like Kazazael, the magician who served Queen Elfa of Commoral, for instance, or even of Zordanor, for that matter.

"I must defend my city against Tor Domnus," she said simply, walking where he gestured, to seat herself on an X-chair. She threw open her robe, revealing her body clad in the scantiest of black gossamer, under which her nudity, might be glimpsed.

With a faint smile, she watched the mage scan her loveliness. He was too old for fleshly desires, she thought, but no one ever really knew about such things where a magician was concerned. She was glad now that she had donned this dark flimsiness that showed so much of her beauty.

"Tor Domnus is a greedy man," the magician admitted.

"He seeks to conquer Kor. He may not stop with that. He may want all the Haunted Lands for his own, including even this black tower and the great magician who lives inside it."

Mindos Omthol paced back and forth. His long cloak flapped to his stridings and it seemed to Zordanor, who eyed him closely, that the hundred signs of the demons of Alpalomnia fluttered and writhed as if alive. When he came to a bronze amillary, he halted and leaned his elbows on a bronze band.

"Xixthur," he said suddenly, and Queen Candara started.

"Xixthur is the cause of Tor Domnus leading his warriors against Kor. So the demon voices tell me."

Candara glanced about her fearfully. Demon-queen she might be, for her father was Hasthar, who lived in one of the eleven hel-worlds and visited her from time to time as he had visited her mother before her, though not in such an intimate way. It had been Hasthar, centuries ago, who had brought Xixthur to her, so that she might live forever.

"Azthamur stole Xixthur from me," she whispered.

"And you would have him back—safely?"

"Yes. Without the threat of Tor Domnus hanging above my head! Tor Domnus knows that Xixthur will give eternal life, and wants my god for his own."

"I too, would like eternal life."

Candara drew a deep breath. "I will—share—my god with you, magician. If you help me drive Tor Domnus away."

His grin was wolfish. "I could take Xixthur away from you, you know. A mere sharing is not enough."

Her back straightened. "What else is there? Would you deny Xixthur to me?"

"By no means. You shall keep Xixthur in the little alcove of your bedchamber. But the man who shares your bed of nights will be me, your highness.

I am sick of loneliness. I would go out into the world again.

"I would be king in Kor!"

Zordanor gasped, leaning forward from the shadows to study the dusky face of his queen. Candara was a woman jealous of her queenly rule, of the city that paid her its allegiance. She would never share her throne with such as Mindos Omthol, let alone her bed. Candara liked young lovers.

Her soft laughter rang out. "But Mindos Omthol, you are old." His smile was mirthless. His scrawny neck shot forward so that he seemed to Zordanor like a hungry vulture about to feast on female flesh.

"I am not so much older than you, Candara," he snapped. "Indeed, I do—believe you have a few years on me, say four or five centuries. It was long before my time that you were born of a princess of Vanda cia and the demon Hasthar. Long before my time."

His laughter cackled in the air. "You have remained youthful for—how long has it been?—surely more than a thousand years. Xixthur has done that for you, Xixthur the god. Xixthur could do he same for me. I will be youthful and strong. You will be happy to have me in your arms on cold winter nights."

Candara made her face smooth. She did not want to offend this old man, even by a facial grimace that might let him know his presence would not be welcome in Kor. No, she must pretend, she must agree to all his suggestions, until the threat of Tor Domnus was no more.

Then she could deal with Mindos Omthol. "I would be happy to share my crown with such as you, magician," she said, "And who knows? With you beside me, perhaps we might extend our rule to that of Urgal, and beyond Urgal into Phalkar and Sybaros."

Her lips smiled a promise that her heart denied.

CHAPTER FIVE

Kothar came to the gates of Kor a little before sunset. Beside him, Philisia drooped on the back of the little mare. It had been a long ride from the ancient chapel of Randolphus, her body ached from the tip of her toes to the top of her brown head. She ran weary eyes over the stone walls of Kor and told herself that Tor Domnus would take this place within an hour.

A guard challenged the barbarian, but Kothar merely pointed to Xixthur strapped on the back of the brown horse and the guard's eyes widened in awe as he nodded and gestured them through.

Kothar called down, "Keep your eyes open, man. Tor Domnus may be on my back trail with his soldiers."

Then the Cumberian toed Greyling to a canter and rode through the cobbled streets of Kor. He would find lodging first for Philisia, he did not feel easy about bringing her beside him when he faced Candara. She was worn with traveling, her shoulders drooped and rounded, her face was streaked with dust and grime.

He avoided the Queen's Navel to draw up before a door set between two jutting bay windows, with tiny panes of glass between their lead grips. There was a courtyard beyond it, through a wooden archway, and candle-lights gleamed in a number of the upstairs rooms.

He half-lifted Philisia from the saddle, her legs were almost too numb for walking, but his arm about her waist guided her until she learned the use of her feet and could stagger beside him into the common room and to the scot counter where a beefy man made figures in a ledger.

A room for the Lady Philisia and a hot meal for them both was soon arranged. They dined below stairs in a corner of the common room, watching it fill with traveling merchants and traders, with some of the city guards, with men and women from nearby houses.

Kothar walked with her up the walled staircase and waited until she was safe behind a latched door before he turned away to find Queen Candara. Suspicion and distrust were strong in the barbarian Now that he had Xixthur for her, would Candara of Kor honor her promise to him, to reward him with a kingship?

He was expected at the palace wall-gate. There was a heavy guard on duty, and as he cantered Greyling across the fountain square toward that wall-gate, the big oaken doors swung wide to admit him. Her magician could have alerted her as to his coming, he realized.

He dismounted in the inner court. His were the hands, that undid the fastenings that held the metal god, his the hands that lifted Xixthur, carried him up the outer stairs.

Candara waited for him in her throne room, dark except for two towering candles on either side of the ivory and ebony chair that was her throne in Kor. Her legs were crossed under a clinging white tunic with a golden belt about its middle. She had loosened her black hair so that it made an ebony waterfall across her bare shoulders down as far as her knees. The white tunic was like a nightrail, something which she might wear to her great four-poster bed of nights. It was of sheer Vandacian linen, which was as thin as the webs of Oasian spiders. Under it, the queen displayed the perfection of her dusky body.

As his footfalls echoed with hollow thumpings in the dark hall, she broke into laughter and clapped her hands.

"You have done well, barbarian." she cried, uncrossing her legs and leaning forward, staring at the thing he carried.

He set Xixthur down with a thump before her.

"I fought Azthamur for this. I left him bound and gagged, and barely escaped from Tor Domnus's soldiers."

She nodded. "You have done well, Kothar. You deserve to be rewarded. And rewarded you shall be!"

She came off her throne, and as she passed before a tall candle, Kothar saw by its pallid light that beneath the white tissue of her gown, she wore nothing at all.

As if to test the prohibition of Afgorkon he asked, "Shall I be prince in Kor?"

She was standing beside Xixthur, running her palms over his smooth metal surface. Her eyes lifted to touch Kothar. "Of course. I have given my word as queen. Gold and jewels, a crown for your head. You shall make a splendid prince, Kothar."

She sounded convincing enough. And yet there was a laughter in her eyes that told the barbarian she toyed with him. To drive out that laughter, he growled, "Tor Domnus comes after me, to take back Xixthur."

She nodded. "I know. Zordanor has warned me."

"I saw no guards on the city walls, only a few men before the gate. Tor Domnus will bring a thousand mercenaries with him."

Gandara clapped her hands. From the shadows four men came, slaves from the Southlands below Oasia, naked to their middles. They bent and lifted Xixthur between them and carried him from the throne room.

Kothar stirred, scowling. He did not trust this queen and her wanton wiles. She should have been worried about the army Tor Domnus was bringing with him from Urgal. She had perhaps five hundred cutthroats wearing her leopard livery; surely not enough to defend Kor for very long, even if they were all fanatic in their loyalty.

He said, "I have some experience in leading men in battle. I would help defend Kor for you."

Her eyes smiled at him. "And you shall, my barbarian swordsman. But not this night, not yet. Zordanor informs me that Tor Domnus will not come to Kor until the morrow, a little before midday. Until then, we have the night and what is left of the morning to ourselves."

She came close, putting her arms about his neck and her body to his, lifting her lips for the kissing. As his mouth closed on hers, Kothar told himself she was a witch, that she knew how to fan the fires in a man's bloodstream with her wiles.

"We shall go to our royal bed, Kothar," she whispered, and put her arm in his.

He walked with her up a flight of stone steps covered with red carpeting to a long gallery. Despite all his suspicions, so sensually alluring was Candara in her white tunic that he found himself laughing as she laughed, whispering words of adoration for her beauty.

Her red mouth was a moist fruit promising ecstasy. Her shoulders, bare above the gown, were indicative of the smooth body that would soon be his. Her eyes glowed as they flattered his muscular bulk by telling him silently that his arms would soon be encompassing her nakedness.

And then, still in the gallery, she turned to teasing.

Catching up her tunic skirt she ran ahead of him like a wood nymph fleeing before a satyr. Her laughter and her dusky face turned back toward him over a shoulder, lured him on.

"Come chase me, Kothar—chase me!" She was perhaps twenty feet away, dancing on sandaled feet. She was a succubus that comes in the night hours to test the male strengths of men. She was Salara and Isthis, the love goddesses of Vandacia and Memphor.

With a bellow, the Cumberian leaped forward.

His hands were stretched out for the grasping, his palms itched to stroke her dusky flesh. It was dark in the gallery, there were no torches, only a candle or two to show the way. Even if there had been a thousand torches, Kothar might not have known his danger.

For all he saw was Candara, with her body nude beneath the white linen of her gown, her head thrown back so that her glossy black hair fell behind her almost to the backs of her knees. Her red mouth. was open and she was laughing, laughing, as the trap door opened under his foot.

The gallery floor fell away beneath his war-boots. "By Dwalka!" Kothar bellowed, falling. Candara shrieked her enjoyment of the moment. But now there was no wanton eagerness in it, to blind and tempt, there was merely mockery and a cold cruelty. She had set her royal trap and like the dupe he was, he had tumbled headlong into it! Down he went in utter blackness, and high above his head the trap dropped into place.

He landed on his feet on a sloping stone ramp and tumbled forward, heels over head, rolling downward until he came to a crashing stop on a dry rock floor. He lay a few moments, gasping, his body throwing off the shock.

He waited, blind in this darkness that was all around him. He knew there was life other than himself in this chamber: His barbarian instincts told him so. Ah, but what sort of life was it? Surely it had heard him tumble downward and roll across the floor:

Why did it wait to attack? For it was waiting, scarcely breathing. He must make the first move, it seemed to be telling him. then it would make its rush.

Carefully, silently, Kothar drew his sword. He was sitting, with Frostfire in his huge hand. Slowly he gathered his war-booted legs beneath him; he heaved upward.

Something rustled in the blackness. Sweat glistened on the Cumberian's forehead. Was it 'a snake, slithering so across the floor? Something touched his ankle. Another something wrapped itself about his thickly thewed right forearm. A foul stench came to his nostrils. Stifling an exclamation of disgust, he slashed sideways with his blade, and struck only empty air.

His left-hand went to his forearm, closed down on a long tendril, tugged at it. The tendril stuck, having sucker-discs along its underside. Kothar snarled a curse and his muscles bulged. The tendril came free.

He slashed with his sword. He heard a shrill cry. Then he was moving forward, crouched, cutting at the thing at his ankle, slashing left and right with his sword-edge, blindly. Twice he felt the momentary opposition of something thin and living.

"By Dwalka! Give me a light, you gods of Cumberia!"

There was only darkness. And now in angry haste, came a score of those tendrils, darting unseen through the darkness, to wrap about his entire body. Kothar was raised upward off his feet, hung there in the air as more and more of the tendrils slipped about him.

He fought savagely to keep his sword-arm free. The thing that had him struggled just as fiercely to enwrap his arms, but it was wary for it knew the right arm held a sharp something that could hurt it. Its wariness was the one weapon Kothar had, for it gave him a chance to slash with Frostfire, to cut free the tendril that held his throat, that sought with its sucker-discs to pull out his eyes.

He felt, drops of ichor touching his skin where the tendrils bled. As he went on struggling, he found that where that ichor touched him, the gripping tendrils slid and slipped.

Kothar twisted himself feverishly now, wriggled and squirmed until more and more drops rained on him. He found a sliced-off section of the thing and rubbed its oozing end over his face and throat, then over his sword-arm until the tendril he held went dry.

In its struggles, the thing that held him discovered that by gripping him tightly in many spots, it could tug at him, draw his arm away from his shoulder, his legs from his trunk, about which it had twisted other tendrils. Kothar knew he was being pulled apart. The pain was agonizing, but he had suffered agony before.

71

He was half a wild animal, and a wild animal bore its hurts with stoic calm. Kothar gritted his teeth and endured that torment of torn flesh and bones twisted out of their sockets. For now he was able to see a thin membranous thing that crouched on the floor and extended thin feelers upward to where it held him suspended above it.

An octopus? A Kraken out of the ocean deeps? No. This was no animal but—a plant! The plant glowed faintly in the blackness, probably a gift from Nature itself, as the deep-ocean fish are provided with lights to show them the ocean floor. The plant was filled with phosphorescent liquids, that ichor which covered parts of Kothar as he battled.

When he has first dropped here, his eyes had been used to the brilliance of the world beyond the trap door. Down here, in this ebon darkness, it took a little time for those eyes to adjust so they could see light as pale as that phosphorescent glow.

Yet now he could see!

With a bull below, he slashed sideways, through tendrils. Up and down his sword-edge went, and now the plant mass below was emitting more, of those faint, shrill cries of pain.

It sought to protect itself, drawing back its pseudo-pods, seeking to cover its membranous mass with those feelers, as a man will try to cover his head against attack by lifting his arms. It let go of the barbarian; Kothar fell heavily to the stone floor.

But he was up and leaping, Frostfire swinging. A dozen tentacles fell away before his attack, until the pulsing middle of the plant lay exposed. One good thrust into its living center might finish it. Kothar panted harshly, swinging up his blade. Then he halted, thinking. Of what good was it to slay this thing? It could not harm him, now he could see it."

"Can you speak, foul excrescence?" he shouted. The thing whimpered. Kothar asked, "Is there a way out of here?" A voice touched his mind. When keeper comes, door opens. The thing was silent. Then: Not harm me, I help.

Kothar nodded, went to sit in a dark corner of the chamber. By the eerie light of the plant, he saw a stone-walled room, in the middle of which lay the glowing organism. The sloping ramp down which he had tumbled was to one side. In a section of the stone wall, Kothar made out faint lines that suggested there might be a stone door hung on big hinges there.

It was through this door that the keeper would come. Kothar put his stare on it, and held it there.

After a time he asked, "How are you named? How did you come here to do Candara's bidding?"

Long time here. Always. Candara find me. There was a pause. It took the plant a long time to marshal its knowledge and put that knowledge into its telepathic signals.

Candara build room. Give food. It grow. A pause. Call it Thyllu. Thyllu eat all. Candara feed.

The plant thought no more at Kothar. They shared this chamber for a little while, then the man would be out and on his way. The Cumberian sat with his sword across his knees, waiting patiently as a wolf might wait for food along a trail. Many hours passed, and the stone door remained closed. Kothar supposed that the keeper believed the plant to have feasted well on the barbarian, the plant would not be hungry for a long time.

He himself was ravenous. It had been many hours since he had tasted food. He would eat when he had left the chamber of the plant. In the meantime he would fight his impatience and his hunger as he had fought the plant.

He dozed a little; it was easy, in the blackness. When his eyes opened, the plant had stretched its remaining tendrils to the wall around the door and above it. It waited as patiently as did Kothar for the coming of the keeper.

Catlike, the Cumberian came to his feet and stepped close to the wall.

He did not stand here long. By some developed instinct, Thyllu must have sensed the coming of its keeper.

The door swung inward. A blazing torch was thrust in. At the same time, tendrils dropped to wrap about the arm holding the torch, and tugged.

A little man, shrilling obscenities, was pulled inward Thyllu so maneuvered him that he could not see the barbarian.

Kothar slipped out into a narrow corridor. He ran. He was in the cellar-ways of the palace, he knew soon enough. His nostrils caught the scent of food from the basement kitchens, and he angled his run so that he came to an open doorway that gave into a wide room where meats were roasting and bread stuffs were baking. Several young girls, with aprons twisted about their slim middles, were attending the ovens and the braziers.

Kothar did not hesitate. Food was before him, and he was like a starving animal. He raced in, snatched at a turning leg of beef and at two golden loaves of bread just off the baking slabs, A girl turned her head, catching sight of him. Her eyes opened and her jaw dropped.

Then her eyes rolled up in her head and she crumpled.

Kothar leaped over her on his way for the farther door. He did not know why the sight of him had in spired such terror. It was good that she had fainted. Unconscious, she could give no signal.

Two other girls saw him and fell to the floor. Kothar raced on, up stairs and along empty corridors. Finally he came to a room with a single wooden door. This he entered, bolting the door behind him.

And then he froze. A giant monster stood facing him, covered over with green stuff, which matted his hair and streaked his face and painted his mail shirt and kilt with ghastly flecks of green.

Kothar growled and raised Frostfire. The giant imitated his action, and Kothar realized he was staring into a mirror. Laughter barked from his lips. "By Dwalka! No wonder those girls were frightened. That green ichor's turned me into some kind of man-beast!"

He sat down on a chair and, lifting the leg of beef to his strong teeth, began tearing at it. He ripped great chunks of meat from the bone, chewing with delight. The meat was savored to a nicety. Those girls were excellent cooks. The bread, too, was sweet to the taste and satisfying to the belly.

Kothar ate until there was only a bone remaining. This he tossed aside into a corner, rubbing his forearm across his lips. He would have given much for a beaker of ale, because thirst was a living thing in his throat, clamoring for satiation.

He shook himself, staring about him. This room was part of the tower base, that had been fitted out with a table and a chair, probably for the use of the guards. A lone window, bisected by a single bar, was set high up in the stone wall. It was a narrow window, but even a man

74

the size of the barbarian might squeeze through it, once the bar was removed.

Kothar pushed the table against the wall below the window, vaulted up on it. Carefully he examined the seating of the bar, found that the masonry was cracked and in disrepair. His hand brought out his dagger and he began prying with the point, dislodging bits of stonework.

Within minutes, he had freed the bolt holding the bar in place on the stone sill. A push of his hand swung the bar to one side. Hoisting himself up, Kothar wedged his shoulders into the opening and shoved outward.

His head thrust through the window, he stared down at a stake-filled moat, then upward at windows glinting golden with candlelight in the night darkness. Between his window and those higher in the tower were a series of crude carvings, placed there for ornament by some unknown mason centuries ago.

Kothar put out a hand, closed his fingers on the carving of a gargoyle. His iron fingers tightened. Slowly he slid his legs out the window and caught hold of a stone leopard's head. His warm muscles swelled as he lifted himself upward by sheer strength.

His toe fumbled for a hold. He loosed his right hand, reached higher for another carving. With toes and hands he worked his way up the face of the rounded tower, until he was hanging below the first of the lighted windows; staring inside.

At first he did not understand what it was he saw. The room was dark, but lighted by strange red and blue and yellow shafts of light that moved this way and that, forming little patterns of purple and green that mingled with the others in a color dance, making the barbarian dizzy. Not until his eyes became accustomed to that pattern did he realize that he was also seeing portions of a nude female body that was bathing in the shifting rays.

Queen Candara was laving herself in those healing rays. She was turning, arms high, crooning deep in her throat, as her flesh gathered the medicinal powers of Xixthur deep within its tissues. The Cumberian grinned. Aye! Let her keep forever young, if she wanted. Let her delude herself and play the fool, not knowing that her fate rested in the big hand that fumbled for the dagger at his hip as Kothar shifted position.

One swift throwing of his knife would end the life of the queen. She could atone for her betrayal of him as the lifeblood oozed from her wound.

As he drew back his arm to make the throw, the metal scabbard holding Frostfire grated across a stone carving.

Candara opened her eyes, stared right at him. Kothar cursed and tried to hurry his movements. Pinned as he was just beyond the window, with a sixty foot drop onto sharpened stakes in the moat below him, he was a dead man if the queen screamed and there were guards within sound of her voice.

"Aiiiieeee!" Her wail woke echoes in the most distant corner of the castle. It made the door from her bedchamber into his alcove burst open with a crash as two men in mail shirts fought to get inside.

"By Dwalka!" Kothar swore, and hurled the dagger.

But Candara was bending, reaching for a wrapper, and the knife whisked past her head to thud into a wooden beam. At the same moment both the men-at-arms brought out their swords and lunged for the barbarian.

Kothar flung one glance below him at the stakes embedded in the moat bottom. Then his war-boots were pressing hard on the stone sides of the round stone tower and he launched himself off the wall like an arrow from the bow.

He went outward and downward.

Somebody shouted for archers, behind him. Below him the stakes were coming up fast to impale his body. The barbarian had sought to angle his fall so that he would land on the far edge of the moat, where the wooden stakes jutted outward instead of upward, to delay attackers seeking entry into the castle. He was going to miss those stakes and land on—

No, by Dwalka! He had timed his fall almost to perfection. His feet went down onto the rounded stakes that jutted away from the castle and he slid backward toward the pointed stakes. His hands scrabbled at slippery wood from which the bark had been peeled, seeking to stay his fall.

An arrow thunked into a stake, a foot away.

Then his fingers, were tightening, his slide was being slowed and then stopped. A man without the sheer animal might of the blond barbarian would never have been able to brake that slide, but the Cumberian managed it—though his palms stung and bled where splinters had rammed into him from the pressure of his hand grip.

Ignoring the pain of his hands, he pulled himself up and over the points and dropped on the far side of the moat. Arrows were falling all around him now, but the archers could not see too well in the starlight, and within seconds the Cumberian was dodging behind a house, racing into a cobble-stoned alley.

He ran for many minutes, until he was at the city wall.

For his steel thews it was a relatively simple thing to leap onto a sloping hovel roof, run to a slated house roof and from the peak of a chimney, jump upward until his hands caught the stone wall capping. He drew himself upward, hooked a leg on the wall-top, and jumped down the other side.

Bells were clanging in the castle. Like a wolf, Kothar loped off into the desert. Once out on those barren grounds or hidden in the misty regions of the Haunted Lands, no man from Kor would ever be able to find him.

Oh, he was safe enough, the barbarian knew. But it rankled inside him that he had failed so ignominiously to blood his dagger in the soft flesh of Queen Candara. Not only that, he had left Philisia to her mercies if the royal bitch learned the woman was in her city.

The Cumberian could imagine the tortures Candara and Zordanor would inflict on Tor Domnus's former mistress if they laid hands on her. And there was nothing that he could do about it.

Raw fury pulsed inside the barbarian as his war-boots made soft sounds, padding along the pebbled pathway that would bring him deep into the heart of the Haunted Lands. His fingers opened and closed to make mighty fists with which he beat the air.

Somehow—he must find a way to even his score!

CHAPTER SIX

He ran on through the thickening mists of the Haunted Lands like a coursing hound, knowing no fatigue, no tiredness in his rolling muscles, only the savage bite of defeat and the fierce need for vengeance. Candara had betrayed him! Candara had gone back on her royal word, she had gulled him instead of rewarding him!

He would make her pay!

By Dwalka, he would!

He was so lost in his thoughts and roiled emotions that he ran headlong into two soldiers in the boar's head uniforms of Prince Tor Domnus before he could halt his run. His weight bowled them backward, but not before they caught a glimpse of his hard brown face and shaggy blond hair.

Their howls were loud and piercing.

Kothar pulled Frostfire from the scabbard, but other men were joining their voices to those yells. "I've stumbled into the vanguard of an army—Tor Domnus's army," he rasped.

He whirled and ran, but now they were calling his name and arrows began flying blindly through the mists. Two hit his chain-mail shirt and bounced off, a third scratched a red furrow across a bare forearm.

But Kothar was running for his life, and he soon outdistanced the shafts. He could still hear their voices calling to one another, and the deeper growl of a sergeant bellowing orders to spread out and link hands.

They meant to take him here in the white fog and carry him captive to Tor Domnus for punishment. To his surprise, Kothar found that Frostfire was naked in his hand; he had forgotten to sheath it. His grin was cruel! Let them come, then. He was ready for them.

He ran on, listening to the calls going back and forth.

The prince himself was galloping forward, eager to be in on the capture. Kothar heard his voice crying out warnings to his soldiery that if they failed him, he would flay the skin from their bodies.

Two men came out of the mists to one side. Kothar gave them no chance to cry their warning. He leaped and his sword flashed wetly in the mists. Its edge sheared through chain-mail and flesh and the man sagged. The second man lunged at him with his own blade, intending to take any reward Tor Domnus might give by wounding this man himself.

But the mercenary had never fought a man like the Cumberian, who was in front of him one moment and three feet away the next. Steel rang out as Kothar parried a vicious stab at his belly.

The clang of the steel echoed across the misty plain. It was like a clarion call to the men who marched with the prince of Urgal. Voices bayed in triumph, and there was the sound of running feet.

The barbarian sprang forward, Frostfire glinting. His first blow drove the man reeling backward as it caromed off his sword-blade and hilt. His next sliced through chain-mail into warm flesh. The man opened his mouth to call for help and it was then, as the first mewling sound came out, that Frostfire's point took him in the throat.

It was too late to run. The harm was done. A dozen men were on top of him, blades ripping the air. Kothar parried and gave ground, but the odds were too many. He could not fight a dozen men at once, unless his back was against a rock. He turned and fled like a deer, his eyes hunting a boulder big enough to guard his spine.

An arrow dug into his thigh, but he ignored it. More arrows were sliding through the mists. One hit his left ankle, piercing the skin but falling off. Kothar ran harder, knowing the exertion was causing his heart to beat the faster and his wounds to bleed even more, but knowing also that to remain and fight would mean capture and an agonizing death by torture.

He lost the twelve men behind him, but they were coming on, able to follow his progress by the drumming of his war-boots on the rocky ground. The barbarian considered removing them but the sharp stones underfoot would cut his feet to ribbons.

Kothar came to a big rock and turned. He set his bearskin cloak to the wet stone and waited, grimly determined to die here in these mists with a hundred foes already dead before him. There was no escape, he knew that; he must have some rest or bleed to death. Frostfire was ready in his hand. All he wanted now was enemies to slay.

And they were coming... oh, yes! He could heart heir voices as they advanced slowly through the fog, calling to one another, keeping in touch.

Ah, but wait!

There was another sound he could hear. It was faint and seemingly far away, but it grew louder, louder, and Kothar remembered that squelching sound he had heard on his way to Kor and he called to mind the memory of the awesome beast he had seen through an opening in these same mists.

"By the gods," he breathed. Squelch, squelch, squelch. Now over those sounds, as three-clawed massive feet were put down in soft mud and lifted out, he could hear the vast breathing of the unknown monster, which was like a gigantic forge bellows worked by a giant smith.

Just beyond the rocks were the marshes of Xanthia, an unexplored region of Yarth where, according to rumors, only strange beasts and monsters dwelled. Kothar could smell their dank stench as the wind shifted.

Kothar jammed his spine against the boulder and waited.

A mercenary came through the mists. He saw Kothar and slid to a halt on the wet rocks. He lifted his head and bellowed, "Here, over here! This way. I've cornered the barbarian against a big rock."

He ran forward, but stopped just out of sword-stroke distance. The Cumberian snarled in his throat. The man was so tantalizingly near! To leap away from the rock, to blood his blade in his body, to leap back! He might kill this lone man, but the slaying would not help him, all things considered.

The others were coming now, moving from the mists into the open space where he stood. Kothar drew a deep breath. They were forming a battle line, advancing on him, shields up and swords ready.

Tor Domnus himself was reining in his white warhorse, laughing to see the barbarian about to make his last stand. In his fine armor and with his glittering helmet, handsomely carved and with a horsetail as its crest, he made a martial figure.

"Disarm him only," the prince shouted. "I want him alive!"

Squelch! Squelch!

The sounds were fainter, as though the monster tiptoed. Kothar grinned mockingly at Tor Domnus on his fine white horse. Didn't the fool or these idiots who passed for soldiers hear those noises? Were they not curious as to what manner of thing could make them? In another moment

The ground shook under his feet. The huge boulder rocked. The sound—the bellow of insensate fury which the monster was emitting through its gigantic jaws—was like a titanic thunderclap. Even Kothar froze motionless, and he had been expecting that frightful trumpeting.

The soldiers of Tor Domnus turned to statues. Their eyes were suddenly enormous, their mouths were open. Not a man moved against Kothar, not a man stirred by so much as a muscle twitch.

Only their eyes spoke for them, turned upward in the mists where a—something—towered high above the head of the barbarian. Kothar caught the stench of the beast now, it was very close, it was visible to the awed mercenaries to whom it must have seemed like a creature out of a nightmare. Clumps of weed and marsh grass were plastered to its grayish scales. It stank of rotted vegetation and of bits of decayed meat. Its breath was as the miasma of a poisoned pond.

Scales and claws grated on rock as the monster advanced.

Then a shadow touched Kothar and, glancing up, he beheld the long scaly neck and lower jaw of this behemoth out of Hell. Teeth glinted as the jaws opened.

A soldier screamed.

The vast head darted downward. Those jaws closed down on living flesh, on half a dozen men. The jaws closed and bones broke as flesh was ripped open and blood flowed out. Kothar shuddered. By the gods. He wished no fate as this on anyone, even on his enemies

If he could have saved them, he might have leaped forward. But his barbarian soul was awed enough to hold his body motionless. In his race memory there was a hint of some such creature as this, and others like it whom his people had fought, long and long ago, and which should be dead yet still lived.

The monster gulped its meal and ate again.

The spell was broken, now. The men who still lived turned to flee, screeching out their terrors. They drove back into the mercenaries, behind them, from whom the monster was hidden by the mists. These soldiers, thinking only that their companions had been terrified by a single man—Kothar—cursed their contempt and sought to pass the cowards and get at the barbarian with their swords.

The result was chaos. A muddle of snarling, angry men, some of them terrified witless, fought to break free of one another. As a result, they were bunched together as the beast came forward, head downward and jaws agape, to gather in those men with a single bite.

A clatter of hoofs told where Tor Domnus fled for his life on the white warhorse. He alone was mounted, he alone could race away from the scaled thing that was eating his men. The hoof-beats receded into the mists, and faded away.

Kothar saw a giant three-clawed foot descending toward him as the monster stepped over the boulder. The only thing that saved him, he realized, was that big rock against which he had placed his back. The thing had not seen him, its attention had been caught and held by the line of men before him.

Kothar flung himself sideways. The huge foot planted itself on pebbles, then lifted as the beast went on, drawn by the screaming, fleeing men who threw away shields and swords and ran to save themselves from such a death. A cry was halted in mid-sound. A man screamed and screamed—and was silent. The crunch of teeth on mail and human bones, the drip, drip, drip of blood from grinding jaws to the ground, were horrors against which he closed his ears.

The stumbled to his feet, tiny against the titanic bulk of the scaled monster. The tail alone must be more than forty feet long! It quivered and shook and when it lashed sideways, the barbarian was certain that the beast would kill him. But apparently the tail had shifted for the purpose of maintaining balance, for the thing did not turn on him but went on after the fleeing soldiers.

Kothar raced off into the mists. He had no goal, he just wanted to be away from Tor Domnus and his men and put the beast far behind him.

He paused in his running to snap the arrow-shaft still protruding through his thigh, and cast the parts aside. He made a crude tourniquet, fastening a length of material from his kilt and knotting it.

Now he walked until his muscles wearied. He lay down to sleep on the moist stones, enduring the dampness and the cold like the half-savage he was, happy that he was still alive. Thoughts of vengeance on

Queen Candara buoyed his spirits, though he saw no way of accomplishing that revenge. Alone and wounded, what could he do against the armed might of Kor?

When the mists grew pale, he knew it was dawn. He walked on, hearing only his own footfalls in the uncanny silence of the fog. He did not know how long he strolled, but he came eventually to the end of the mists and walked boldly across the barren ground.

Toward noon, he saw the cross in the distance.

A man was tied to the cross by wrists and ankles. In front of him, half a dozen desert wolves were crouched, feral eyes fixed on the helpless thing that writhed there. Kothar strode forward. Whoever the man was, he was human. The wolves could wait for a different meal.

His savage shouts and the glint of Frostfire as he waved it drew the famished beasts toward him. They were used to seeing a man on foot, they viewed him as a meal. The cross that had been set up in the rocky ground and to which the man had been lashed was new and strange to them, and so they had waited, studying it until certain it was not a trap. Then they would have attacked.

Kothar slew three of the wolves and wounded the others, until they turned and fled from his bloody blade. Then the barbarian turned and walked toward the man. To his surprise, he recognized Kylwyrren.

The magician smiled through his pain at sight of the Cumberian. His white-haired head inclined in a little bow. "Greetings, man of the north. We meet again."

A dagger slashed the ropes that held him prisoner to the crucifix. The old man sagged and would have fallen except that Kothar put his arm about him and eased him to the ground.

"I have no water," Kothar growled. The magician shook his head. "There is no water behind the mists, in this hellhole. But perhaps in the camp that Tor Domnus abandoned there may be a canteen or two that some terrified soldier threw away."

The old man chuckled. "Something must have frightened the prince very much. Was it you?"

Kothar spoke of the scaled thing that had come out of the marshes in time to save his life. "I do not know what it was. It was huge. It ate half his army, I think."

"I have heard tales of such beasts that dwell in the marshlands of Xanthia, though I have never seen them, not even in my crystal ball." His pale hand lifted and gestured. "Can you carry me, barbarian? To the abandoned camp? It may be that I can help you in your quest."

The Cumberian lifted the old man easily. As he stalked along, he asked, "What do you know of my quest?"

"I peered into the ball for Tor Domnus. I saw you fall into your trap in Candara's palace. I saw your attempt to kill her. I watched as you fled into the mists. Now you seek revenge."

"She owes me a reward. Let that reward be her life!"

"Kor is a very strong city. It has many men-at-arms inside its walls. Even such a warrior as yourself can never hope to walk into it and work your will of its queen."

Kothar confessed his puzzlement and his hopelessness as far as any chance of gaining his revenge on Candara was concerned. It was in his mind to take leave of the Haunted Lands and seek his fortune elsewhere.

"There is a way," murmured Kylwyrren, but he would say no more until he was in the abandoned camp.

Here he found a carafe of fine wine, abandoned by Tor Domnus who had thought of nothing but escape from the strange monster that had come up out of the marshes of Xanthia to eat his soldiers. There was food too, hastily thrown aside for swifter running, and weapons and rich brocades and even chests of jewels and coins.

Kylwyrren and the barbarian feasted until their bellies swelled, sitting on the X-chairs that had also belonged to Tor Domnus. The magician had gone to the ground where his tent still stood and peered in side, nodding his head in satisfaction when he beheld that his magical accouterments were undisturbed.

"Tor Domnus had other things on his mind than taking my properties back with him to Urgal," he told Kothar. "Besides, he attributed all of his troubles to my failure as a mage. My magicks were not strong enough to ward off such evil as had befallen him in these barren lands, and so he crucified me, expecting that wild animals would slay and eat me, and he would be rid of me forever."

Kylwyrren sighed. "Could he have forgotten so soon that it was my magicks—the necromancy he appears to hold in such low esteem—that first brought Azthamur to Urgal and his service? That it was my enchantments that held the demon ensorcelled so that it must serve him as my prince willed? Well, I know ways to remove those necromancies! Ah, then will Tor Domnus rue the day he left me to die on that cross."

"Azthamur is dead," Kothar protested. "I slew him."

The magician cackled laughter. "You bested him in a fair battle, barbarian. No more. You slew his humanoid-fish shape, true. But the demon Azthamur you could no more slay than you can slay the mists you see low on the horizon, yonder.

"No, no. Azthamur lives, waiting to serve me. Though not in the fish-man body in which he appeared to you. He shall have his own shape now, as I send him after Tor Domnus. Here, give me a hand."

The barbarian loaned his great strength to the tasks imposed on him by Kylwyrren, for the mage had promised that, when his own vengeance was a thing accomplished, he would make certain that Kothar should have his. He carried heavy metal, alembics and reliquaries from the tent and set up a little bronze altar on which Kylwyrren might offer incense and pour libations to the demoniac being that served his will.

He stood close beside the mage when he did these things, for the necromancer warned that sometimes these beings out of the nether worlds did not understand such things as friendship, and one or another of them might well eat him in a thoughtless moment or carry off his soul to whatever bottomless pit he made his world. The barbarian was restless and uneasy while Kylwyrren chanted and made his magicks, he would rather have been on a fast horse galloping through one of his northern forests, but he made do with this new friend because of what Kylwyrren had promised.

He handed Kylwyrren the golden rod with which the old man drew his pentagram, making it large enough so that Kothar might stand inside it with him.

"For Azthamur is a vengeful demon," Kylwyrren explained, "Seeing you, he will want to rip your soul from your body and carry it off to the hundred hells where he dwells in his demon shape. I would not want that to happen, nor would you."

85

Kothar moved his broad shoulders uneasily. Though Kylwyrren assured him with a smile that it would do him no good against such as, Azthamur, Kothar drew Frostfire and held it in his hand as the old man began his incantations to the demon of Urgal. A wind had come up during the night that blew little dust devils, around his feet and made him bury his chin deeper in the folds of the bearskin cloak that guarded his throat.

Then, as Kylwyrren chanted faster, the wind sank away and an utter stillness came upon the land. The sky darkened slowly, it grew overcast and gray, and underfoot the ground trembled. More and more that stretch of rock and sand quivered, until it ran like jelly in a bowl. Kothar was hard put to maintain his balance, though the magician himself seemed untroubled.

Kylwyrren exclaimed worriedly, "There is something wrong! Never before has Azthamur behaved in such fashion! Azthamur—Azthamur! I summon you up in the name of the thousand and one demons who are your brothers and your sisters I call on you in the name of the arch-fiend Nabbadon himself!"

The ground quieted but the wind commenced to moan, ruffling the bearskin cloak that Kothar wore. The air hushed. Then a thunderclap came close to breaking eardrums as something black and polymorphous appeared inside a blaze of brilliant scarlet light.

No shape had Azthamur, that black blotch that hung between Yarth and sky, it was quivering sentience, alive, sinister, evil. Its very evil beat out at the mage and the barbarian in waves of nauseating fury.

"I am here, magician!" The voice was mere whisper, filled with hate and the lust to slay. The blackness bellied as if troubled by a strong gale, Tiny red eyes opened in that blackness and glared hard at the Cumberian.

"Him I want, Kylwyrren! Him I must have before I do your bidding. Send him out of the sacred pentagram to me."

"Forget your feud with Kothar," shouted the mage. "I offer you a different victim—Tor Domnus, prince of Urgal."

"Aye...Him I mean to have also, in my abode. But first the barbarian."

"Not so. Tor Domnus is your victim and I adjure thee by the rites of evil, by the eleven incantations to Salara, by the—"

"Enough! enough! I hear your voice, old man!"

"Then begone about your business."

"I shall yet come for him! Hear you! Azthamur, enemy? I shall come, I shall come—when I have done with Tor Domnus!"

The blackness swirled, faster and faster, until it was no more. It disappeared so swiftly that Kothar grunted and blinked his eyes to the hot sunlight that poured down on him as a result.

Kylwyrren was grave, thoughtful as he gathered up his appedimenta. "I do not like this, Kothar. Azthamur has an unholy hate in his demoniac soul against you. He will not rest content until he has come for you, dragged your soul from your body and drawn it down to his lair in the hundred hells." Kothar growled, "I fear no man or demon."

"You'll do well to worry about Azthamur. Never before has he been beaten. It irks his pride. His injured pride will not let him rest until it has been salved by the sight of your spirit writhing in some agony of his devisement."

The old man shook his head. "I fear for you. There is no enchantment that can keep you safe, no amulet to wear about your neck. I did not suspect Azthamur felt so strongly, or I might not have summoned him up. But once I did so . . ."

He broke off and walked across the ground toward his tent. Kothar rumbled anger in his throat, following him, arms laden with the altar. He was not afraid, he did not know what fear was, but he admitted to a sense of uneasiness, being honest enough to doubt that Frostfire could kill such a being as Azthamur.

When his gear was neatly placed within the tent, Kylwyrren turned to the big barbarian. "You helped me, Kothar. It is my turn to help you."

He bent and lifted a shovel and placed it in the hands of the Cumberian. "Stand you here beside me, on this bronze plaque containing the sigil of Nabbadon himself."

Kylwyrren began to chant and the outlines of the World around them shimmered, grew gray and hazy. When the mage was done, the shimmering disappeared and when he stared about him, Kothar saw that they were in the foothills of a nearby mountain range. He did not bother to ask the old man how he had accomplished such a miracle; it was enough for him that they were here.

The white-haired magician pointed at the ground. "Dig here, Kothar!"

And Kothar dug, until he had uncovered a marble slab three feet down. He growled, glancing up at Kylwyrren inquiringly. The mage smiled, nodding.

"Lift the slab, barbarian," he murmured. Kothar bent, fitting his powerful fingers into the space between the slab and the stonework below. He grunted, tugging. The slab was heavy. Heavy! But great was his strength and as his back muscles bulged, the slab lifted, slowly and steadily, until the barbarian could set it on end and stare down at what was revealed beneath it.

"By Dwalka—a tomb!" he breathed. Kylwyrren nodded. "Yes, a tomb. Here lies the greatest of the warriors of ancient Vandacia. His name was Aywold the Wise. He is covered now by a sheet that rots in the dampness of the ground. Remove it."

With his sword-hand, Kothar yanked away the rotting stuff of a funeral shroud. His eyes stared down at the skeleton of what had been an immense man, clad in link mail from head to the boots on his feet. The link mail was rusted, as was the hilt of the sword in the decaying scabbard, and there were scraps of hair here and there on what had been a face, once on a time.

Kylwyrren made gestures with his hand, chanting. The dead body and its accouterments quivered, shimmering as the air had shimmered and the barbarian choked back a curse. The body below his feet was changing, taking shape. The rust spots were fading, the armor and the weapons were brightening. Flesh came to clothe the bones of the long-dead Aylwold and the hairs of his beard turned a reddish brown and fluffed out until—

Eyelids opened. Pale blue eyes stared up at the barbarian. This was no lich! This was a living man below his war-boots.

"Who are you, man?" asked Aylwold. "Kothar of Cumberia. And I think I have a need of you!"

"Sharp wits, barbarian!" cackled Kylwyrren. "Indeed you do have a need for Aylwold the Wise. I have brought him back from the Other world where his spirit dwells—to offer you both the gift of vengeance accomplished."

Kothar put a hand down. Aylwold clasped it, let the Northman yank him upward until he stood uncertainly on his own feet. Aylwold grinned, staring down at himself.

"I live again, as a man. By my sword, I'm not sure whether I'm glad to be here or not. The Other-world has its advantages, old one. Still, I heard you speak the name of Candara, whom I hate for what she did to me and my companions, and to satisfy the need for revenge in me, I will listen to your words."

Kylwyrren spoke swiftly as the Vandacian listened, nodding from time to time and shouting with admiration as the mage told of Kothar's fight with Azthamur and how he had taken Xixthur out of Urgal, and later how he had escaped the trap Candara set for him.

He swung on Kothar, a big man and wide in the chest, wearing old-fashioned armor but even more dangerous in appearance because of it. His long reddish-brown hair-blew in the wind off the wooded slope behind him, and his hand curled lovingly about the braided hilt of his long-sword

"A good tale, man. I envy you your deeds. So Candara built her city, did she?" At Kothar's exclamation, he grinned. "Aye! Tis the same Candara, on my hilt. Long has the demon-queen lived. Long, long! It's time she died, barbarian. Let us go together and slay her."

"Not so fast, howled the magician. "There are your companions to be raised from their graves. Would you deny them a taste of their own vengeance on the woman who poisoned them all?"

"Not I. It will be good to see the Ten, again."

"Stand you on the bronze plaque, Aylwold." It was a tight fit for three men, especially since two of the men—Kothar and Aylwold— were big of chest and wide of shoulders. But they managed it and the air shimmered around them, seeming to press them closer together and the foothills went away and in their place—

There was an island, bordered by reeds and swept by a damp breeze that held the smells of salt water and tiny woodland flowers. The wind that rippled the surface of the marsh-waters was chill, raw. Kothar shook himself and glanced at the magician.

"A queer place to bury the dead," he groused.

"Centuries ago, the marshes had not come so far inland," Kylwyrren answered. "There was water close by, true, but this was all dry land, then."

"I mind this place," Aylwold growled, looking about him. "Over there—those stones half buried in the loam. They are blackened, you'll note. It was at a campfire ringed by those stones that Candara poisoned the Ten while I was off on a hunting trip." He sighed and stepped off the plaque, reaching for the shovel Kothar held. "We were of the Royal Guard, and I was their captain. King Calyxius had sent us with his sister Candara to make sure she stayed far away from the borders of his land.

"Candara had a thousand men and women with her, the riffraff of the world, the scum of Yarth who flocked to her evil banner. She wanted us dead, that none might return to Calyxius to inform him of her plans."

The shovel hit into the soft dirt. Weeds and dirt and flowers flew in huge chunks as the Wise One worked. He began to speak in rhythm with his tool.

"Me she slew as I entered her encampment, two days march north of here, laden down with dead deer and boars for the feasting. An arrow out of the darkness, without warning. Like that!" He dug the shovel deep.

Kothar dropped into the hole Aylwold had made, bent to tug free a root. Below him a number of bodies lay entangled in their common grave. These were the Ten, great warriors all, Aylwold assured him. They were the Royal Guard of Calyxius and in Vandacia during those days when he had been alive—Aylwolds informed the barbarian—only the mightiest warriors of Yarth could be taken into such a select company.

But —

"Ten men against Kor?" Kothar wondered, uncovering a mailed hand.

Aylwold barked laughter. "Ask Kylwyrren, barbarian."

The magician smiled. "Those ten are as ten thousand, Kothar. Be not alarmed. Join them in the brotherhood of fighting warriors, and go about your destiny in peace."

They rose from their grave, ten huge warriors in link mail as old-fashioned as that which Aylwold wore, skeleton figures in rusty armor as they lifted up in answer to the ringing words of the magician. But as they stepped onto the ground, out of the pit, they fleshed out and their armor grew bright and new.

One by one, they came forward to meet Kothar and greet their old leader. Fandlon and Ibanar, Kasthin and Morillon, Petrolix, Aberthan, Nixol, Judkin and little Ilthur who had a wooden bow hanging from a shoulder.

They were hard-bitten men, they had the look of warriors. There was confidence in their bearing and in the manner in which they swung their weapon-belts about so that their swords were closer to their hands. They looked at Kylwyrren in curiosity and listened gravely as Aylwold the Wise explained why their spirits had been called back from the Other-world and their bodies made young and warlike once more.

"We are your men," Ibanar said to the barbarian. Little Ilthur unslung his bow and tested its catgut string. "Long has it been since I pulled at The Slaughterer. Ah, it feels good to hold his length and fit an arrow to his string!"

His laughter rang out, loud and happy. The magician said, "Come! Azthamur is about his business and there is no time to waste, if Kothar is to slay Candara. Gather you on the plaque—yes, yes! All of you, I said. The plaque can hold you all."

The bronze plaque grew as the mage made hand motions above it. Soon the Ten, with Aylwold and Kothar and Kylwyrren, were on its surface and the island under it was shimmering with haze and disappearing from their view.

There was a thump. The shimmering went away and before their startled eyes were the walls of Kor, the outlaw city. Above the wall-tops they could make out the leaded rooftops gleaming in the morning sun and see the flash of armor where a guard strolled back and forth along the wall-walk.

Kothar stepped off the plaque, followed by the others, who paused at the sight of this city that had been no more than a dream in the mind of Candara when she had murdered them. It was now an actuality more than a thousand years old. Kothar turned to Kylwyrren who was shaking the dust off his robes. "My thanks, mage. But ten men against Kor?" Kylwyrren chuckled. "Worry about Azthamur, not Kor and

Candara, Kothar! You shall see the wisdom of my words before long. But now—farewell."

The magician and the plaque shimmered into invisibility.

Kothar grunted and turned his face toward Kor. There ahead of him was his enemy, that traitress demon-queen who had used him and then sought to slay him in an abominable manner.

Kothar began his walk toward Kor.

CHAPTER SEVEN

Metal clanked beside him as the Ten and their leader walked to his striding. To his left was Ilthur with his longbow in his hand, to his right was Aylwold, his sword in his right hand. None of them had shields, and the breezes that whipped dust from the plain across which they walked also rippled the hairs on their unhelmeted heads.

A horn blared somewhere behind the walls. Men ran to close the great gate, for there was something grim and terrifying about the way in which Kothar and his warrior friends walked that alarmed the men and women inside the city named Kor. They had seen them materialize on the empty plain, they knew magic and necromancy were involved, and they were fearful.

The men in link mail did not hurry their strides. There was no haste in them, though Kothar himself seethed and sweated in a rash of impatience. At last he said hoarsely, "Those gates will be closed when we get there. We'll never get inside Kor then!"

Aylwold chuckled. "Be at ease, Kothar. We men of Vandacia have strange ways, now that we are dead. Strange, strange ways!"

Ilthur laughed softly, raising his bow. "I am almost within arrow range, Aylwold. Suppose I announce our intentions by feathering a shaft on yonder fat man leaning over the parapet?"

"Better to use your arrows on the men at the gate, Ilthur Remember, we have no siege engines, and we cannot climb such a tall wall without ladders."

Ilthur drew back his bow, held the arrow poised for flight. There was a twang of catgut and the shaft flew with blinding speed—unreal speed, Kothar saw, since his keen eyes could not follow its flight through, the air—until it thudded into the chest of the fat man at the parapet.

A wail went up from inside the city. "No man can shoot like that!" the barbarian grunted.

Ilthur smiled faintly. "I am no man, barbarian—not anymore. I am a spirit living inside a body made by Kylwyrren's magic. There is a— difference."

They walked up, seeing the wall-walks fill with archers bending bows, stringing them. Moments later they were standing in ranks, bows up, arrow-points aimed at the oncoming twelve. At a shout from their captain, those bowstrings twanged and the air filled with arrows.

Kothar ducked; his sword turned two shafts. Beside him, Ilthur never moved. Three shafts hit him—and bounced off Aylwold on his other side chuckled with grim mirth.

"Aye, barbarian! Eleven we are in number, but as ten times ten thousand in effectiveness. Being dead men already, how can we be killed? And Kylwyrren has made our flesh like iron, that will turn any arrow, any sword-edge. Now do you feel better about matters?"

They walked on, link mail chinking to every stride. Kothar told himself that he was mortal if the others were not, and that it behooved him to be careful in the fighting that was coming, lest he be slain before he could run steel into Queen Candara. Then he grinned. By Dwalka! He had never fought carefully in his life. He was not about to begin now.

Ahead of them was the gate, closed and bolted.

Aylwold snapped an order to the others and ran forward, passing Kothar. As they had done at other times—hough carrying a bronze-headed ram between them—the ten sprang forward, following their leader. They ran swiftly, with awesome speed. They came closer to each other as they ran, so that they were shoulder to shoulder, bared heads lowered.

Kothar gasped, "Fools! You'll knock yourselves silly!"

They never heeded him but ran on, always more swiftly. Now they were within the shadow of the gate overhang, now they were hitting the great gates with their lowered heads, like men turned into rams. The gates splintered, crashing inward under that one great blow. Wood tore off iron hinges, chips of hard oak flew through the air.

Kothar was running too, waving Frostfire.

His throat thickened with the battle lust. By all the gods of war! These were comrades to fight beside! As the gates went down he could look into the city itself, where the cobbled square stood, and see men running to fight the invaders whose blades were out and whipping left and right.

Only Ilthur stood back a little, whipping arrows to his bow and firing them swiftly. His shafts always found their marks, digging into mail and flesh and dropping men in mid-stride.

Kothar was beside him, cutting down a man with a war-hammer in the act of swinging it.

Ilthur laughed, "My gratitude, Kothar—but there's no need to protect me. No weapon can harm this body of mine. Go you on your way, and leave the taking of the city to us!"

Ahead of him, Aylwold was cutting down guardsmen and mercenaries with every thrust and cut of his great blade. Fandlon and Petrollix swung battleaxes side by side with Nixol and Judkin whose hands were wrapped about the long hilts of their swords as they slashed and slew. Aberthan and Ibanar, Kasthin and Morlon fought, with blades in their right hands, stabbing daggers in their left. And as they fought, they chanted a song that was as old as Vandacia itself.

We say, we warriors of the East, man and woman, child and beast,

For any who oppose our lords—must die before our bloody swords

The chorus of that song rose upward, swelled and grew into a pulsing rhythm that seemed to drive fear into the ears of their enemies just as much as did their dripping blades. Chanting, moving forward with every step covered by the body of an enemy,

Aylwold and his Ten advanced across the cobble-stoned city square.

Kothar did not wait for them. No man was he to let another do his task. And his task now was to find Queen Candara and slay her. Aye! Before the demon Azthamur came for him.

His, teeth showed in a savage snarl as he hurled himself forward, Frostfire cutting a path for him with point and edge. Men dropped before his blade, men shrank from the glare of his battle brightened eyes. In moments he was through the thin line that opposed him, running swiftly down a street. He went past the Inn of the Queen's Navel with a single glance at its closed windows.

Philisia was somewhere inside that inn, but he had no time to spare for her. Candara was on his mind, and it was only her face he wanted to see at the moment.

There were no guards at the open gates of the palace wall. They had been summoned to the city gate to repel the attack of the madmen who had appeared out of thin air. He ran into the courtyard, glanced about him at the silent, still bulk of the palace.

"Candara!" he bellowed. "Demon-woman—I've come back for you!"

Lightly he ran up the narrow stair, bursting into the room with the heavy brocade draperies and the hooded hearth. The room was empty. Sweeping aside a hanging with a hand, he ran easily up the narrow stone stair revealed to his eyes. Candara had her bedchamber somewhere up above him, and it was there he would corner her and drive steel into her flesh.

He came onto a broad landing that he recognized as part of the round tower in which the demon-queen had her bedchamber. This door before him, this wooden thing with painted signs upon its planked surface, was the door into her room. Kothar put a hand on it, pushed inward.

The door held. The barbarian shoved a shoulder against it, pushed. The door did not budge. Kothar grinned coldly and stood back. He swung Frostfire in a vicious sweep, saw the cold steel bite, into the wood and bluish fire spring to life, which signified that there was magic in the wooden door which the bite of the magic sword was freeing.

Again and again he struck, until the door was a splintered thing barely hanging on its iron hinges. Then Kothar raised a war-booted foot, kicked hard.

The door went inward with a crash. Queen Candara stood in the middle of her bedchamber, sandaled feet planted inside the red lines of a pentagram. Her cheeks were flushed, her eyes brilliant with hate and fear.

"Stay back, Kothar!" she shrilled. "Or you die!"

He laughed harshly and leaped, and the demon-queen raised her arms and cried a single name.

"Azthamur!" There was no reply to that lone scream, and now Candara shrank and would have run but Kothar was on her, sweeping her into an arm and carrying her across the room with him, slamming her back into a draperied wall.

"You die, woman," he whispered, and lifted Frostfire.

His eyes touched her face, saw the exquisite, dusky beauty of the long-lashed black eyes, the red mouth that was like a fruit and sweet to the taste of kisses. The demon-queen wore a clinging garment of black samite, that showed the curving lines of her body, and revealed the length of a shapely leg where the skirt was slit for greater ease of movement. Then his gaze slid to her soft warm throat. There, where the pulse beat showed beneath the blue-veined skin, he would slash with Frostfire's edge! Then Candara would perform no more of her wickednesses on Kothar the barbarian-swordsman!

She stirred a little in his grasp. Their ears could hear the howls and screams of her soldiers and her citizenry as the men from their ancient graves stalked through the city, slaying as they went. Her long lashes quivered as she stared into his hard eyes.

"No need to slay me, Kothar," she whispered. "There is no need of hate between us. Remain in Kor with me. Be my king, my prince!"

His left hand that gripped her upper arm shook her savagely. "There can never be anything between us, Candara. Once—before you sprang that trap on me—it's true I thought about being your consort. But no more!"

"Call off those ghouls you brought from their graves, or there won't be any city for either of us to rule. Listen to me, Kothar! I was a fool. I admit it freely. I did not appreciate what a man you are."

His sword came up. He turned it so its keen edge lay an inch from her soft, pulsing throat. Death glared back at her from the blue eyes into which, she stared, and she shuddered, for the demon-queen was afraid. Yet she spoke bravely enough, chin high in defiance of his steel.

"The gold and jewels of this part of Yarth can be yours! Together we will attack Urgal, make it our city!"

He chuckled, remembering Azthamur. No wonder the demon failed to answer the ringing call she sent him. He was too busy slaying and feasting in Urgal to bother about Queen Candara and the spell she must have been making, seconds before he broke in on her.

He growled, "As Azthamur failed to answer your call, so do I!"

He thrust the Sword Frostfire forward. Its edge never touched her flesh. There was an invisible barrier before her which even Frostfire could not penetrate. The muscles of his right arm swelled with his effort, but the blade never moved.

Candara smiled slowly. Kothar felt the tension ease from her flesh. He rasped, "What demon protects you now, woman? Or whose spell is it that keeps my steel from drinking your blood?

Zordanor's?"

She shook her head slowly. "A greater mage than he, by far. Have you ever heard of Mindos Omthol, barbarian?"

Unconsciously, Kothar eased his clasp of her arm. She freed herself gently, as if not quite daring to test his rage again. Her left hand came up to massage her bruised flesh where already a black and blue mark marred its whiteness. Her black eyes blazed triumphantly at him.

"I went to Mindos Omthol, Kothar, threw myself on his mercy! He vowed to help me, and he has. You cannot work your will on me, man of the north. You're helpless!"

"Not quite, by Dwalka!"

He swung his fist at her middle, but it seemed he tried to hit the wind. Something caught his huge fist, held it motionless, inches from her belly. And the queen laughed softly.

"Try again, barbarian!" She stood proudly, defiance in her every line. For a long moment they confronted one another, warrior and demon-queen, until a lassitude came upon the big barbarian and the weight of his sword grew heavy in his hand so that he was forced to lower it.

"You shall come with me to the magician," she said softly. "With his help I shall conquer Urgal which is a greater city than Kor. Tor Domnus we shall put to death and I shall rule in his place."

"Tor Domnus is a dead man," he replied dully. "Azthamur went to him and ate him or whatever it is that demons do to men they hate. As he will try to do to me, I suspect—in time."

Her laughter was triumphant. "Foolish Kothar, who thought to defeat Candara! You are no more than a living dead man, now. Mindos Omthol has laid a spell on you, by which you must obey my whim."

It was true enough, Kothar thought glumly. There, was a

sluggishness in his flesh and a dizziness in his mind, so that he could scarcely think for himself. Somewhat clumsily he sheathed his blade and then looked at the demon-queen.

A part of him understood that he was under a spell and fought against its hold. But it was, a fight that he knew he could not win. An untutored barbarian from the Northlands could never hope to defeat such a magician as Mindos Omthol! Yet he must make the attempt. Even as lethargic as he was, as helpless to fend for himself, he must find a way to conquer.

"The alcove, Kothar Lift Xixthur, carry it for me."

He heard her words dully, as from far away. Where she bade him, he walked, entering the alcove, seeing his dagger still stuck into the wooden beam where he had thrown it at Candara. He bent and his big hands went about the metal bulk of Xixthur. He heaved upward, lifting the metal thing to his shoulder.

That which it had taken four men to carry here, he supported easily. He turned and stared at Candara. She went ahead of him to the door of her bedchamber and led the way down the staircase. But where she should have walked straight ahead, toward the gallery overlooking the courtyard, she turned aside.

Her hand fumbled at a stone carving. With a faint rumble, hidden machinery purred to life, and a stone section of the wall slipped back revealing a narrow tunnel. Into this the demon-queen stepped with Kothar on her heels.

The stone rolled back into place, shutting off all light. Candara reached behind her, caught the barbarian's free hand.

"Follow where I walk. Take no step to left or right that I do not take, for there are hidden pitfalls here."

He followed as might a man in a dream.

They came at last to a small door which Candara opened. Stone steps ran upward to a trap door. This Candara lifted, and came out onto a stretch of pebbled ground some hundred yards beyond the staked moat of the castle.

She stood a moment as Kothar joined her, the wind whipping her black samite garment, staring at the walled city of Kor. There was a flush of anger in her dusky cheeks, defiance in the tilt of her chin as she listened to the sounds of slaying coming from behind those walls.

"Over a thousand years I ruled in Kor, barbarian," she whispered. "And now my reign is at an end." Her eyes slid sideways to touch him and the Cumberian marveled, even in his bemused state, at how much hate he could read in her glance.

"I owe my defeat to you!" she snarled. "But you shall pay. Oh, yes—you shall pay. Between us, Mindos Omthol and I shall conceive of a punishment to fit your deed. Be assured of that."

She turned and walked away and Kothar followed as might a dumb beast of burden. They walked for miles, until Kor seemed far away, and then the barbarian saw a misshapen thing standing at a small hovel, with three horses saddled and bridled for the riding. Zordanor came forward at sight of them, moving with his crablike gait.

"You did not slay him, highness?"

"Azthamur is in Urgal, taking vengeance on Tor Domnus whose whims he obeyed so long as the spells of Kylwyrren held him in thrall. Now Azthamur is free."

Zordanor shuddered and made in the air the sign of Huldor, who is a beneficent demon. He bobbed his head and peered around him as if expecting to see the lord of the hundred hells rise upward from the ground itself.

"It behooves us to ride for Mindos Omthol, highness. He alone possesses the power to protect from such as Azthamur."

She nodded and moved toward a white mare. The hunchbacked magician advanced to cup his hands for her sandaled foot so that, she might the more easily mount into the high peaked saddle. Then he hobbled toward a blue roan and raised himself into the saddle.

"Mount you also, Kothar," smiled the woman cruelly. "I would not have you worn and exhausted when we come to the tower beside what used to be the Sunken Sea."

She touched her horse with a toe and moved out across the barren lands. Zordanor came after her, turning in his saddle to watch Kothar, balancing Xixthur on his shoulder, rise up into the saddle of a rawboned bay. The bay sidestepped under the weight of the barbarian and the metal thing, but the strong hand on the reins and the voice of its rider calmed its fears.

The little cortege wound through the Haunted Lands, traveling over rocky ground and through the misty lands, skirting the great marshes of Xanthia until the barbarian could see the tower where resided the magician Mindos Omthol, rising upward on the rim of a downward slope where once had rolled the waters of the Sunken Sea.

As he rode, the Cumberian had fought against the strange spell that held him, but fruitlessly, so that he seemed still to be in a dream, unable to move or even think for himself. He accepted what happened because a deadliness of spirit lay inside him, and he had not even the desire to fight back.

It was as they paced their horses slowly through the mists that they heard the faint shuffle of unearthly feet, as though some awesome beast or demon were creeping through the fog, hunting for its prey. Candara reined in, smothering an outcry, Zordanor huddled his mount beside hers.

Kothar alone seemed unaffected by that sound, so alien to their world. He sat his saddle gripping Xixthur by a mightily muscled arm, but he looked neither to left nor to right, not even when the demon-queen stiffened and Zordanor crouched down inside his cloak at sight of the black, polymorphous thing they glimpsed where the mists roiled and parted. In that clear space for an instant, they saw a living embodiment of unutterable evil. Zordanor spoke the word, "Azthamur!" But he spoke it silently and under his breath so as not to attract the unwelcome attentions of that demon which quested here and there for they knew not what.

No pentagram had Candara and Zordanor to protect them, and both queen and magician sensed that Azthamur would not be particular about what souls he feasted on. They sat their saddles in an agony of terror until the mists came together and hid the dark demon from their eyes.

Long they stood there, hardly daring to breathe. Not until a full hour later, after Azthamur had gone on his way, did they dare to move. Zordanor leaned forward, whispered to his queen. And Candara nodded, pale of face and quivery of hand, as she lifted the reins and shook them so that her white mare might proceed along the way to Mindos Omthol.

Almost in silence, they continued on their journey. And so they came at last into the shadow of the tower and heard the metallic voice of the brass figure boom a greeting at them. Candara slipped from her saddle, casting a triumphant glance at Kothar.

"Step down, barbarian," ordered the demon-queen. "We are at the end of our journey."

The barbarian did as directed without feeling of any kind. He stood like a dumb beast with the metal thing on his shoulder until the doors of the tower opened and the brass man emerged. Up to Kothar he marched and took Xixthur away from him and walked back into the tower with him.

Queen Candara and Zordanor followed. At the sill, the demon-queen turned and beckoned impatiently to the Cumberian. Kothar walked toward her, unable to do anything else.

Up a spiral staircase they went, until they came into the room where Mindos Omthol worked his thaumaturgies. The old magician stood tall and regal, his eyes blazing beneath bushy white brows, his thickly veined right hand tightening and loosening on his long robe. Gravely and with dignity he greeted Queen Candara and Zordanor, and with great curiosity, turned his stare upon Kothar.

"So then, this is the barbarian who has served me so well. I am sorry I was forced to place a spell upon him, but I could never have brought you here with Xixthur without it."

Candara dismissed the Cumberian with a wave of her hand. "He has performed the task you set him, mage. Let us dispose of him."

Mindos Omthol smiled at Candara. "Not yet, great queen. Not yet. I may have a need for this Kothar."

He turned toward the queen. "Turn on this metal machine of yours, if you please. I would bathe in its rays."

Candara advanced across the room, bent to touch the metal object with a finger. Instantly the lights sprang to life behind its lenses, shooting outward across the figure of the old man as he stood and let his robe slide to the tiled floor. Across his sunken chest and skinny thighs those beams of light played. To the dazed Kothar who stood watching all that took place with dull eyes and enthralled mind, Mindos Omthol seemed a gargoyle figure of a man, painted red and blue and yellow by those lights.

Long did Mindos Omthol bathe, and across his face was the shadow of a fatuous smile. When he was done, he reached for his robe and slid into it. Then he moved across the room and gesturing Queen Candara and Zordanor to him, stepped inside the red pentagram on the stonework floor.

"I shall summon up Abathon out of his dwelling place amid the ten hells of Kryth, now. Stand you within the holy lines with me." For an instant, the magician stared at Kothar, then made a sudden decision.

"Step you forward also, barbarian. Otherwise Abathon will think you surely to be a sacrifice for him."

Kothar did as he was ordered, silently.

In his quavery voice, Mindos Omthol, began to chant, even, as his gnarled old hands swung the golden censer and Candara pressed closer to his gaunt frame.

Within moments there was a rustle as of dried leather and once again the demon Abathon stood inside the tower room. Two red eyes stared at the magician, then turned to look at his companions.

"I have bathed in the rays of Xixthur, Abathon," shouted the old man, triumphantly. "That which we planned for me to do, I have done. I shall grow youthful and strong, and with this woman here, Candara of Kor, we shall rile this corner of Yarth that is known as the Haunted Lands."

A wicked chuckle broke the silence that followed. "Fool that you are, old one! Did, I not warn you? I can give you your lost youth now—and I shall. But I also warn you—this youth will last but for an hour and may never again be duplicated!"

"You lie," shrieked Mindos Omthol. The demon-queen smiled sadly. "It is true what he says, great mage. I know the powers of Xixthur only too well. He can maintain youth if one possesses him. He can prevent you from aging—even at such an age as you now possess. But he cannot make you young and keep you young!"

Mindos Omthol staggered back a step. His hand, questing for support, touched the iron-hard muscular arm of Kothar. His eyes under their shaggy brows turned toward the young giant.

"Not to be young again . . . after all the years I spent in my quest of Baithorion's lost secret . . . I think my old heart will stop!"

Suddenly Mindos Omthol stiffened. "Wait Abathon—listen to me!

There is another incantation—that of a transference of souls! I mind Baithorion himself is said to have used it from time to time, to experience pleasures denied to his real body!"

"True. Baithorion possessed such a spell."

"I have it here, in the parchments my agent found for me in Anthom. I shall perform it, with your help!"

Abathon was silent for many moments. At last his red eyes blazed. "It is true. With my help and that of the spell of Baithorion, you may transfer your spirit into that of any body you choose—"

"And I choose this body," yelled Mindos Omthol, slapping the bemused Kothar on a shoulder. "And do not tell me this transition is temporary. I know better. It will, endure. My spirit shall be in the barbarian body, his spirit locked in mine—or all Time!"

"Yes, if I—slay your old body with the spirit of that barbarian inside it," the demon admitted.

"I order you to slay it, when my spirit is in it."

"I hear, mage. I shall obey." Kothar raged and fought against this dread sentence, deep inside him. He was aware of what was happening, but his body did not belong to him any longer, it was under the spell of Mindos Omthol. His fingers would not lift to lock about the hilt of Frostfire, his legs would not carry him so much as a single step, so that he could flee from this ensorcelled tower. He was forced to stand like any dumb beast and hear his sentence pronounced, his eyes compelled to watch the ceremony that would put his spirit into the scrawny old body of the great magician.

Mindos Omthol reached for a parchment, unrolled it and began to read its words in sonorous tones.

Abathon rose upward, began a strange dance in his eerie manner, at the same-time chanting words in a language no human tongue could pronounce. Candara cried out, shrank against Zordanor.

Kothar felt light, airy. He was being freed from the grip of flesh and blood, he saw the walls of the room recede and turn to bluish haze. He quivered there, between his powerful body and the space around it, helpless to do a thing.

He wanted to yank his sword and lay about it, to slay this magician and the demon-queen and her own mage so that he would be safe, but he could not touch even his body, so ethereal had he become. He hovered above his motionless flesh and saw, to his left, that there was a glowing nimbus rising from the body of the old magician.

Now he was being swept forward across the room on his way to the body of Mindos Omthol, while the spirit of the mage went past him to inherit his own body.

The thundering words of the old magician appeared to rock the tower to its very base, and at the same time they drew him down inside the scrawny body that had belonged to the great mage. In moments, Kothar felt himself trapped within that ancient bag of bones.

The parchment scroll dropped to the floor. The body of Kothar, with the spirit of Mindos Omthol inside it, drew itself up to its full height. A happy cry burst from the beardless lips.

"I am young again. Young! Stronger than ever I was when I was a youth. Gods of Yarth, I feel vibrant, quivering with strength. My thanks, Abathon—my eternal gratitude!"

"Pay the sworn price," cried the demon. "Send me your old body and the fresh young spirit inside it. There will be little blood in your still—living corpse—but what there is, I would have!"

Kothar felt hands placed on the bony body which he now inhabited, hands that shoved him forward to the rim of the pentagram and beyond it so that he stood unprotected against the red-eyed demon who paused to savor this moment of its triumph.

Kothar found he could now lift his skinny arms about which the sleeves of his cabalistic robe flapped loosely. With them he tried to ward off the oncoming demon, knowing in his heart that even if he possessed the strength of his real body, it would not have been enough.

And then—all movement ceased.

At first Kothar thought the spell—which had been broken by the transference of his spirit into the body of the old magician-a-was upon him once again. But even the demon Abathon did not move, and as Kothar rolled the rheumy eyes of Mindos Omthol, he saw that the old man—yes, and the demon-queen as well—were just as motionless as he.

Something black oozed along the topmost step of the spiral staircase that led down into the lower floors of the tower. It ran slowly, slowly, and the old heart that now belonged to Kothar lurched with an awful terror.

This was Azthamur, coming for his spirit!

No longer did he adopt the guise of fish-man. Instead the demon was in its own natural casing, a black polymorphousness that might assume any shape it cared to take. Right now it was an oozing excrescence of evil, sliding up the stone stairs and across the room.

Horror etched Kothar, in whom was the spirit of Mindos Omthol, into a grotesquerie of utter despair. The spirit of Kothar laughed grimly. Well, he would die here this day, but he would drag these others down with him, the magician who had stolen his body, with the demon-queen who had sought to betray him.

Flowing and slithering across the flooring, Azthamur advanced on Kothar. Backed into a corner was the lesser demon, Abathon, red eyes wide in awe as it beheld it's superior in the worlds of demonry. Abathon alone could move yet he, too, was under something of the evil spell that flowed from Azthamur like a mist across the swamps.

To the body of Kothar came Azthamur. Black tendrils slipped upward, along those thickly thewed legs. More liquid blackness crept higher, about the thighs, encasing his lean middle, slipping upward across his chest.

The horror of the moment shook the soul of Mindos Omthol. "I am not the barbarian," he screamed thickly. "I am the magician, the magician!"

"Liar, liar," whispered Azthamur. "The spirit you seek is in the body of—"

"Silence!" thundered the demon. "From henceforth you shall suffer in silence whatever agonies you shall endure in my lair, man of the north Never again shall you speak!"

The body of Kothar was surrounded by utter blackness. A moment it stood so, and then it crumpled, as Azthamur flowed down and away from that limp flesh. For an instant the stupefied onlookers caught sight of the gray something that was the spirit of Mindos Omthol, writhing in pain, struggling for a freedom it would never attain.

The blackness flowed faster and faster. Seeing it leaving, the spirit of Kothar fought as silently and even more fiercely than had the spirit of the old magician, to escape his own prison. He needed desperately to be out of this scrawny body and back into his own. Perhaps the fact that his own body was untenanted, and that it acted as a natural magnet for his soul, helped his struggles.

In a moment he was free of the inert clay of the mage's body and back inside his own. He raised his head, feeling a numbness over all his body. His spirit flowed outward, into fingers' ends and toes, into every section of his heavily thewed frame.

Kothar staggered to his feet. The demon Abathon was coming for him, from across the room. But slowly, as if afraid that Azthamur might discover the imposstiture of Mindos Omthol, and, return. Kothar was standing now, scowling blackly as he watched his doom advance on him.

He said, "We have no quarrel, demon, now that Mindos Omthol is gone. Go your way in peace."

Abathon chuckled. "The magician promised me a feast of blood and spirit, barbarian. I do not mean to leave without it!"

Kothar swung about, his big hands reaching for Candara and Zordanor. His iron fingers tightened on soft flesh and hard bone. He whirled, flinging a screaming Candara from him, so that she slipped and stumbled straight at the demon with the red eyes. Shrieking, Zordanor left his feet and tumbled, rolling over and over until he came to a halt before the grim being.

"Take them in my place," Kothar rasped.

He yanked Frostfire into the light, to bolster his argument that the demon should take substitutes for his own flesh and blood. A moment the demon paused, eyeing that long blade. He sensed the magic in it, and wanted no part of it.

Abathon put a tendril on Zordanor, holding the man still. "There isn't much blood in this one," he complained.

"Ah, but the other!"

Candara screamed and tried to flee but about her was a black loop, holding her still. With her long red nails she sought to scratch Abathon, but only sank her fingers ends into wet black ooze.

"Kothar—save me!" she screeched. "Share my throne with me. Let me be your slave. Only save me!"

His hard laughter rose upward. "What? And step into a trap door again? Or have another such spell put on me as held me thrall to you while you brought me here? No, no, Candara. The farther you are from me, the safer I shall feel. And Abathon will take your spirit far—very far!"

He waited until the demon drew both man and woman into its embrace, until the demoniac blackness had encompassed them. There was only a faint mewling from Candara and from Zordanor, and then no sound at all. In moments, Abathon receded into his ten hells, and of the queen and her personal magician there was no sign.

Kothar growled and shook himself.

He stepped from the pentagram and moved across the tiled floor. There was a need in him to get out of these Haunted Lands where no man could trust another, and the demons seemed to be more malevolent than they had been in Commoral or Gwyn Caer.

He would ride to Kor and find Philisia. Then he would go north with the woman into Phalkar.

END

Thank you for purchasing Gardner Francis Fox's Sword & Sorcery classic: Kothar and the Demon Queen.

Find out more about Mr. Fox by visiting

GARDNERFFOX.com

Made in the USA
Coppell, TX
12 June 2021

57315515R00065